Confessions Of A First Lady

BY

Denora M. Boone

Published by David Weave Presents

Dedication

In Loving Memory

Of

Dorothy and Fred Jefferson

Acknowledgements

We know God is always first to get my thanks because He is the one who allowed me to get to this place in my life. Without Him I can be nothing and with Him I can do all things.

I know how much God loves me because of the man that I have been waking up to for the last thirteen years shows me daily. I love you Byron for always being my comfort and support when I don't want to keep pressing. I thank you for being that constant thing in this inconsistent life we live.

To my babies Jalen, Elijah, Mekiyah, and Isaiah, Mommy loves you more than you can ever understand. There is NOTHING that you could ever do that would make me stop loving you or not be proud of you. I watch you sometimes as you all sleep and just thank God that I have four amazing children that no one could ever duplicate! Keep growing into the wonder young men and woman of God that I know you are.

To my father Bobby D. Jefferson, if there is anyone that loves his daughter's more than you love Shacora and I, I would tell him that he is a lie! No one could possibly love anyone more than you love us! I thank you for being there even when I was being stubborn like you. I've never had you tell me that I disappoint you with any of the decisions that I have made for my life. You are constantly telling me how proud of us you are and that means so much to have a father like you in my life . It may have taken us years to get here but if I had to do it all over again to get these results I would! I love you so much Daddy!!

There are so many people that have recently come into my life and I wonder why God waited so long to do this! I can't imagine what life would be like if you guys were not on this ride with me! Now if I forget some please don't charge it to my heart.

My publisher David Weaver (MB) you are awesome! You continue to hold me down and guide me and I appreciate all of your hard work. You are dedicated to the success of your authors/family and know I can confidently speak for us all when I say we appreciate and love you.

I always thank my sisters Krystal Sheppard and Deja McCullough (she just got married to my lil brother yall!!!! ☺) we got each other's backs til we make it in to heaven! I love my brothers NyQuan and Donte for taking care of you like the amazing women that you are cause if they don't, they already know it's a problem!! Lol

There is no way I can forget my ace boon coons Crystal Reeves, Brandi Nixon, and Bishop Kerry Bernard Smith (yall know I had to do his whole name chile) the three of you take me all the way back to our middle school and Elbethel Baptist Church days and have been here for me through some of the hardest and most triumphant times of my life. I really appreciate and love all three of you cause you keep me uplifted and grounded only like family could. #TippitIsHere ☺

My big sis Fanita "Moon" Pendleton , the night to my day! You have been such a big inspiration and finally I can be the little sis and have someone to look up to. I adore you and thank God for you. You keep me encouraged and don't even know you be doing the Lord's work! It gets no realer than you hunty! High 5 sis!

Yoshi Chance I have no idea when we became related but I swear you the best cuz ever!! Lmbo!! I'm proud of the growth that I have seen in you and know that everything you do I will support you til the end. Shoot if I don't Granny won't be happy!

Author Nicki B!! I remember you being the Squad member that stood out to me cause you didn't like "church folks" and then ended up being my girl! I laugh every time I think about you saying me and your grandma are the only Christians you like even though you be trying to fire me! Thank you for accepting me for who I am as an individual and not a stereotype. I'm gonna go before the Lord and pray for your husband boo!

My readers are the best!! I have really gotten close to you guys and if I can't remember all of you I'm so sorry! I try to respond to each review I receive on Amazon (even the not so pleasant ones) I haven't done a few but I will get back on my job.

Rochelle "Rollie" Petrie you and Mizz Ladi Redd have been two of my biggest supporters that knew nothing about me until I dropped my first book and the two of you have really shown me your hearts and support. I appreciate the two of you and the words of encouragement that we give to each other means a lot. Keep being the beautiful people that you are and I pray God will continue to open the doors that you are requesting Him to open. Just trust Him!

My WHOLE #TBRS family I love yall!!! I may have a different personal relationship with each of you but the love is the same!

It's #ChequeSeason right DW?! I'm all in!!

To everyone else that I may not have called out I love you and don't worry I have more books to put out so that means more shout outs to give!!!

Be Blessed,

Dee

Text TBRS to 22828 to stay up to date with new releases, sneak peeks, and more...

Chapter One

Veronica

When I say service was good today, I mean foot stomping, praise breaking, running around the sanctuary, crying good! I live for those days when people in the congregation get full off of God's word. There is nothing like feeling the presence of His power and love surrounding you.

Let's not get it twisted, though. We have some people who feel obligated to come just cause it's Sunday; You know the ones that raise hell all week long and don't even try to do right but they are sitting on the front row with their prayer shawl and church fan. Don't get me wrong, God can still use them but they have to meet Him somewhere. They just choose not to.

I'm so rude; please forgive me. I'm Veronica Millhouse also known as First Lady Veronica Millhouse of "Clover Hill Church of God In Christ". My husband, Pastor Marcus Millhouse, is the head pastor here and we have over one thousand members that come here to worship. We moved to Atlanta, Ga from St. Louis, Mo almost five years ago with our three children Marcus, Jr who's sixteen, and twins Destiny and Dynasty who are thirteen. We are still getting used to living here, but it's officially home now.

I remember when one morning out of nowhere Marcus woke up and said that God told him it was time. Me having no clue what he meant, I was stuck on dumb.

"Time for what, baby?" I asked as I made breakfast with a confused look on my face. I sat his plate in front of him and stood there waiting for an answer.

"Time for me to start my own ministry. You know God has been dealing with me about this for a long time but He never told me when or where to do it," he said.

Remembering this topic a few years back, I slowly nodded my head but kept quiet as he continued.

"While I was in the shower and doing my morning prayer I heard Him tell me loud and clear that it was time now. He wants us to move to Atlanta and start our ministry there, baby," he said smiling from ear to ear. Who was I to tell him that I felt in the pit of my stomach that something wasn't right? So instead of me voicing my opinion I smiled, shook it off and asked, "When do we leave?"

"Well we are going to make sure that we have all things in order before we leave here; tie up any loose ends with the business and sit down with Bishop Thompson to let him know our plans."

Bishop Thompson was the head of our church home at Greater Mount Zion Pentecostal Church and was all about people succeeding. When Marcus first told him of the possibility of him starting his own ministry, Bishop was as excited as he was.

Our children on the other hand, not so much. We understood it would be a big change considering that they were all born and raised in the Lou, and for a while our girls cried days at a time. But once we took a weekend trip to close on the 4,500 square foot house in Buckhead, they were all in. They would all be starting their new elementary and middle schools after the summer break that year.

Since they had a few months to meet new friends around the neighborhood and at the park their transition into the school was easier. Now they loved Georgia and couldn't imagine living anywhere else.

There was a knock at my door before I saw the handsome chestnut brown face peep in. My son Marcus, Jr, M.J for short, was the spitting image of his father. Our friends and family often joked about me being mad at Marcus the whole time I was pregnant with him because our son was certainly a replica of him.

At sixteen years old, MJ stood a firm six feet one with beautiful almond shaped eyes, a cute button nose, a tad bit of peach fuzz (as I like to call it) above his upper lip and on his chin. The only thing that he did inherit from me was the two dimples he had on each side of his handsome face.

From the day he was born I knew I was going to have to fight the little girls off with a bat, but being that Mark and I had raised him to focus on God and school first he didn't chase everything with a big hump under their backs, if you know what I mean. Sure there were little girls that were interested but he saw how his father treated me and his sisters and knew that having a girl for every day of the week like some of his friends just wasn't for him.

The one girlfriend he had, he met her at church. Lailani was the same age as him and danced on one of our praise dance teams. Her parents Torre and Malachi Abrams were two of our faithful church members and so far she proved to be such a sweet and respectful young lady. Taking these things into consideration, we knew there was some type of solid foundation that she was standing on.

"Mom, Dad said he's closing up his office now and he is pulling the car around front," MJ said.

"Ok baby, I'm coming. Where are your sisters?" I asked as I stood up to grab my purse.

"They are already in the truck with Lailani. Daddy said she can go with us to dinner," he said blushing.

Even after being in a youthful relationship for almost a year I could see that he still felt the same way about her as he did the day they met. I just prayed that they always kept this innocence about them for as long as possible before the world tried to change their way of thinking.

We prayed that by us not tying them down and constantly shoving the Bible and a scripture down their throats every waking moment they had, they would be well grounded. Mark and I knew the stigma associated with Preacher's Kids or PK's and that's the last thing we wanted our children to be.

Of course we had our rules and guidelines that we wouldn't change for anyone like making sure to at least spend twenty minutes out of everyday to just be in God's presence; whether it was praying, worshipping in song or dance, or just reading the Bible. Whatever it was they chose, they enjoyed it and it helped them to build a strong relationship not just with God but with everyone in their lives.

Raising them this way allowed them to be able to make the best decisions for themselves and so far, they have made really good, sound ones. That gave us comfort and cut back on the worrying like a lot of parents had to do.

I closed my office and set out for the front of the church but the closer I get to the vestibule, there is a tightness that comes over my chest. Not like a heart attack or anything, but that feeling you get when you know something is about to jump off. There was definitely a shift in the atmosphere and I couldn't quite make out what it was. The closer I got to the front of the church I could hear laughter. Not any ordinary laughter like someone told a joke, but a more seductive type of laughter.

I paused for a few seconds as I waited to see if the voice and laughter belonged to the same person. As God sits on the throne up high, I prayed I was wrong.

Lord knows I'm trying to take a step, but it feels like my feet are in a bucket of cement and my legs are slowly turning into jelly. My breathing is becoming labored and my eyes start to water. There is no way in hell this could be happening. Not now. Not twenty years later. This was definitely not happening at church of all places.

"Please God don't let Satan be around this corner," I quickly prayed. I guess that prayer didn't make it past the ceiling because as I finally got the strength to ease around the corner, the sight before me confirmed that prayer was unanswered and it stopped me dead in my tracks. As soon as our eyes made contact, the reason Satan decided to make a personal appearance became clear.

Revenge.

Chapter Two

All the way to the restaurant I felt like crying. This could not be happening to me. I'm sure by the way Mark kept glancing over at me every few minutes he knew something was really wrong. His usually happy and vivacious wife was on cloud nine after a powerful service like the one he had ministered today. That's one of the things he knew that I loved about him. There is nothing sexier or more attractive than a man who is after God's own heart.

"Hey babe," he said as he reached over for my hand with a worried expression on his face.

"Hmm?" I asked trying to make as little eye contact as possible.

"Everything alright? You look like your mind is a million miles away."

I tried to muster up the most genuine smile that I could to put him at ease and end the question and answer session he started, so I simply said, "Yea boo I'm fine. Just a little tired that's all."

"You want to just get take-out instead of dining in?" he asked as he massaged the inside of my palm with his thumb.

Lord knows this man is my everything. The simplest touch from him ignites the fire that's been burning within me for the last nineteen years of our marriage.

"No baby, I'm okay. Let's go ahead and dine in. That way when we get home I can focus on something other than clearing dishes, if you know what I mean." I flirted knowing that would get his attention on something else. The smile that reached his eyes let me know he was ready and willing for anything I had planned for later this evening.

******

It was Destiny's turn to pick the restaurant this Sunday and although I had been blindsided just a short while ago, my stomach didn't care - it just wanted to be fed. The Melting Pot was one of my absolute favorite places to dine in and the children loved it just as much as I did.

We enjoyed our meal as a family and before heading home we dropped Lailani off at her house. We waited in the car while MJ walked her to her front door and kissed her cheek.

"EWWWWWW!" yelled the twins out the window. They loved getting a rise out of him whenever he was around Lailani.

"Girls behave," Mark scolded them as he shook his head.

MJ made it back to the car with promises that he would call as soon as he got home.

As we pulled up to our home I thought about where God had brought us from. Days haven't always been sunshine and rainbows for us. There were days in the beginning of our marriage when we didn't know where our next meal would come from or even where we would lay our heads that night. Of course we worked but living paycheck to paycheck wasn't enough. One night as I lay in Mark's arms at one of the local hotels, I could feel the weight of the world on his shoulders.

"What are you thinking baby?" I asked him.

He sighed deeply before answering. "You deserve better than this. I can't even provide a decent, stable place to have my wife. I'm supposed to be a man that can provide stability for his family, not this," he said getting up out of the bed and opening his arms wide while looking around the small room. It wasn't bad but it wasn't where either of us wanted to be.

I walked over to him with the biggest smile I could muster up under the current circumstances, and put my arms around his waist.

"Our time is coming Markie," I said calling him by the pet name I had given him. "We just can't give up. You will never be alone in this world as long as I have breath in my body."

I turned him around to look at me so that he could see the sincerity in my eyes. I placed my arms around his neck and pulled him in close. "Will you pray with me?" he asked. Instead of answering him I took his hand and walked back over to the edge of the bed as we got down on our knees. We needed God and we needed Him now.

"Heavenly Father we come to you right now as humble as we know how, dear God, to ask for your forgiveness. God, whatever sin we have committed known and unknown I pray that you forgive us right now.

Please hear our cry to you, Lord. We know where our help comes from and right now all we have is you. God we know that you have more to offer us in this life and you are not a God of lack. So right now God, we cry out in the only way that we know how and that's in prayer. Open doors that have been closed dear Lord, and close doors that no longer need to be opened. You said that everything that our hands touch will be blessed and no matter what the situation looks like right now in the natural, we trust you to be working it out in the spiritual. Help us to hold on to your word and not get discouraged. Help us to be strong for one another and not faint.

You put me as the head of my household God, and right now I don't feel like I'm doing a good job, but I trust you. I trust that this is not the end of us and you will get the glory out of our lives. We surrender wholeheartedly to you right now Father. Take control of everything and block the attacks of the enemy. Help me to be a better husband for Veronica and an even better father once we have children. Allow them to never have to see a day of struggle in their lives. I trust there is about to be a shift,

God, as I pray to you. I can feel it. Greater is coming and I praise your name in advance. Hallelujah! Glory to God! Continue to move on our behalf so that not only are we taken care of but we are able to help so many of your people. Let our lives be an example of your awesome power, your awesome grace, and your awesome mercy! Have your way in our lives Lord, so that we may please you.

And right now God, I thank you for my wife. Lord, she is truly my help mate and I know she is sent right from you. I know how much you love me by how much she stands by me through thick and thin. I know how much you love me by the love I see in her eyes. I feel the strength being poured back into me and I thank you God. Thank you for always being a way maker. I lay it all at your feet right now, God. In your son Jesus' precious name we pray, Amen."

After that prayer the following morning, Marcus got a call a about a job he applied for six months prior. They were offering him a Computer Systems Analyst position with a starting salary close to sixty five thousand a year. We were able to buy a new home, and a month later we were expecting MJ.

Now here we are eighteen years later living the life that God had set for us. While I should be happy, I'm now scared out of my mind that this could all be coming to an end.

Chapter Three

I made my way up the stairs and headed down the hall to check in on the kids. Destiny and Dynasty are both in their rooms catching up on the most recent episode of the Real Housewives of Atlanta and MJ was tucked away in his room with his iPad on Face Time with Lailani.

Marcus had already made sure the house was secure and went on to bed ahead of me, or so I thought. Making it up to the top level of the house I can see a soft glow under our doorframe and hear one of my favorite songs by KeKe Wyatt called "Fall in Love", playing softly.

"Tell me are you ready for what I got and how I got it planned out,
Tell me that you want it and you can't wait for me to put my hands on you,
Boy you feel that heat all on your body,
And you're waiting on me to get it started and your body's waiting on me.

You can't wait for me to put my hands on,
Your body's calling me, I've gotta handle.
Tell me where and how you want it, (want it)
You don't know the best cause you ain't had me yet.
And when we finish making sweet love baby,
You gon' fall in love with me.
And baby tonight, you gon' fall in love with me (with me)"

I open the door slowly and I'm mesmerized at the sight before me. The bay window that's behind our California King Sized bed is wide open and the evening breeze is blowing softly. Marcus has the area surrounded with my favorite Ylang Ylang scented candles, and the room is full of petal pink roses that he knows I love so much.

There is a flickering of light also coming out of our master bathroom with the door slightly ajar. I start humming along with the song as I close my eyes and slowly sway my hips to the melody. I hear Marcus clear his throat and I open my eyes to see my king standing in front of me with only his basketball shorts on. Even after all of these years of being married, I still get butterflies in my stomach every time I lay my eyes on him.

He's like a statue standing a strong six feet three inches and weighing in at a firm two hundred and thirty pounds of all muscle. Me being only five feet five, loves that I have to stand on my tippy toes in order to kiss him. He keeps his hair in a low cut taper full of waves. The small amount of grey hair he has is just enough to give him that distinguished gentleman look. At forty years old, he is the sexiest man alive to me.

"What are you doing?" I asked sweetly while gazing into his eyes.

"Well you know that I can always tell when you are stressed or something is bothering you, so I wanted to cater to you tonight. Babe, you are always taking care of everyone else and never have time for yourself," he said slowly walking towards me as KeKe sang on.

> *"Baby put your hands on me, 'cause I wanna feel good,*
> *It's the way that you grab my waist in the place that you should.*
> *Boy you know my body is calling your name,*
> *Every night is something new your touch is not the same.*
> *You can be excited, surprised every day*
> *I can't wait for you to put your hands on me baby."*

Marcus reached out for me and I stepped into his awaiting arms. I wrapped my arms around his neck as he pulled me close around my waist. There is a misconception that just because people are saved or they are the head of a church that romance is null and void. That couldn't be further from the truth. If anything it's enhanced because in the eyes of God, the marriage bed is undefiled. Thank you Jesus!

We danced until the song was over and the next one began. He stepped back looking into my eyes and from his soul said, "I love you so much Mrs. Millhouse."

"I love you more Mr. Millhouse," I said meaning every word. That's why I had to prevent my past from destroying the life I fought so hard to keep.

Daley and Marsha Ambrosius serenaded us with *"Alone Together"* as Mark lifted me in the air and carried me towards the bed. Living in the area of Buckhead that we did allowed us to have a beautiful view of the moon and the star filled sky on this clear night. The music along with the candles, roses, and light breeze set the atmosphere for a night full of passion, and more importantly a deeper spiritual connection with my man.

He ran his fingers through my hair as our breaths became one and in sync with each other. Two bodies, one breath. I rubbed my hands up his strong arms until I got to his face and took one of my fingers and traced his lips. I sat up to kiss him and the initial contact was one that took the both of us by surprise.

A connection was so strong at this moment that nothing could come between us. Our Heavenly language began to fill the air and mixed with the faint sound of the piano in the song And movements like a carefully choreographed love dance. He looked down at all of my glory and I smiled at the man before me. We locked our fingers above my head as he caused our bodies and spirits to slowly link and become one.

An hour and a half later we were spent as we lay together wrapped in a sheet on the bed. My mind was back from the depths of pleasure and stuck in a deep pool of worry.

"What's going on in that beautiful mind of yours baby?" he asked me.

This was something that I really did not want to address so instead of answering that question I simply said, "Just thinking of the conference coming up and making sure I have everything in order." I was gonna need for God to forgive me for that lie but right now wasn't the time. I knew Marcus didn't believe me but instead of giving me the third degree he just pulled me closer and kissed the top of my head as we drifted off to sleep.

Chapter Four

"E"

Walking through the hotel door into the spacious room, there was a feeling of being so close to victory that intensified the excitement within. Getting out of these shoes and changing into something more comfortable was first on the agenda. After that, a bite to eat and placing a phone call to the one woman who would lift their spirits even more.

"Hey mama!"

"Well hey yourself. How's my baby doing?" Mrs. Verna asked. She had been waiting three whole days to hear her child's voice. Although she had two other children, this one held a special place in her heart.

"I'm fine. I just left church and before I got ready for work tomorrow I wanted to check in with you. How is everything?"

"Oh everything is fine now that I'm hearing from you. Your Daddy is out back in the garden and Tricey and Justin just left. They asked about you," she said starting to sound weary.

Sucking their teeth they responded, "They don't really care about me, they just want to be nosey and see what I'm doing, that's all."

Before Mrs. Verna could reply there was a knock at the room door. "I gotta go mama. I'll call you back tomorrow. I love you and tell Daddy I said wassup. Bye."

On the other end Mrs. Verna felt like something was wrong; either it had happened or was about to happen, and something was telling her that her child was the ring leader. No matter how hard Mrs. Verna prayed for her youngest child it seemed as if God was ignoring her prayers. There was something deep in her soul that was telling her the move from Chicago to Atlanta on such short notice didn't really have to do with a new job, but she didn't know what else it could be. All she could do now was keep praying and hoping that one got through to the Father's ears. If not, hell would sure be rejoicing in the havoc that was about to play out.

****

"Who is it?" they asked before opening the door.

"You forgot about me already?" the person asked seductively from the other side of the door.

"Never that." Was the response that was given as the door was opened to allow entry.

They both walked over to the small love seat to sit down and get a little more comfortable.

"So what do you have planned for the week?" Adrian asked admiring the glorious sight. God sure did know how to sculpt a masterpiece made of flesh. Everything was right in place on this body and it had to be a sin to be that fine.

That body was the first thing that was noticed when Adrian walked through the church doors during Bible study last week. Once their eyes met it was an instant connection. One thing led to another and a few phone calls later they were setting up a date after church today.

E was too sexy to say the least and knew it without a shadow of a doubt; always have been always will be. So it wasn't farfetched that two very attractive people were drawn to one another. If things went as planned they could possibly be a power couple. Swag was definitely off the charts.

"Well I have to work but I also have to go house hunting. My space is too small if you know what I mean. I hate being in such a small area even if it's bigger than most rooms." True enough this was a luxury hotel suite, but it was still too small. "I want a backyard and no one above or under me at all times."

Something about the way "under me" had been said was making forming a complete sentence nearly impossible for Adrian. They talked and laughed for a few more hours and ordered some room service before it was time to part ways. They agreed to get together later in the week for lunch or dinner before saying their goodbye's.

Although their night together didn't end up with a long love making session, step one of the plan was coming together nicely. Now it was time to focus on step two. Little Mrs. First Lady Veronica would think twice about trying to hide secrets once everything had come out. How dare she think that she could just walk away. It seems that since she got so called "saved," she has forgotten about her life before the cloth. That was okay because she would remember soon enough.

Right now Veronica was looking like the biggest hypocrite, and once her past came out, all of those church folks wouldn't be so forgiving; especially that husband of hers. Obviously she forgot the seeds that she had sown all those years ago, so now she had to be reminded that it was now time to reap the harvest.

Chapter Five

Veronica

"Good morning Mommy," Destiny said as she came down to get breakfast. It was the last week of school and they had so much planned for the family. I had finally convinced Marcus it was time for a family vacation and in just seven days we would be off to St. Croix for two weeks. Everyone was excited especially the kids.

"Hey baby," I said while making everyone's plates. I could hear the cavalry making their way downstairs.

"Good morning," everyone said to each other as Marcus made his way over to me to place a kiss on my lips.

"Eeeewwww!" all three of the kids playfully said.

"Mom and Dad I have something that I need to ask you." M.J. said as he glanced at his sisters. The look did not go unnoticed by me or his father.

"Sure baby, what is it?" I asked with a raised brow.

"Well the girls and I-" he started only to be cut off by Dynasty.

"Whoa playboy! Unt Uh, this was *your* bright idea. Me and Dez just thought it would be fun," she said turning to look at her sister. "Girl he tried it!" as Destiny nodded her head with a smirk on her face.

"Would somebody please tell me and your mother what is going on?" Marcus asked looking down at his watch. He had a little over an hour before he had to be at the church. Just enough time to spend with us before we all went our separate ways for the day.

"Can Lai and Jacobi come with us on vacation? Now before you say no," MJ continued when he saw me and his father try and catch our breaths, "it's not like we will be staying unsupervised in a hotel room; we will all be at the summer house together. Lai can share a room with the girls and me and Cobi in my room," he finished with pleading eyes.

The silence was deafening as the three stood there waiting on Marcus and I to stop talking to each other with our eyes. They never understood how no words could be spoken between the two of us but we were always on the same page.

"We don't see a problem with it," I said, shocking all of my children. "Put your eyes back in your heads," I laughed.

"Really?!" MJ said almost knocking me over.

"But we have to sit down and make sure her parents are okay with it first," Marcus said.

We all agreed as we talked about the trip while we finished our breakfast. MJ couldn't wait to get to school to let his best friend know he would be going on vacation with them. It was more so for Jacobi to be away from his family situation at home, even if it was for only two weeks.

As the kids headed to the bus stop, Marcus kissed me and said he would see me later in the day. We had a counseling session with one of the newer couples at church. Their marriage was still considered to be in the honeymoon stage but it was so far away from paradise. Hopefully with the experiences that we had gone through in the beginning of our relationship and the first five years of marriage, we would be able to help them hold on to one another.

****

It was close to ten in the morning by the time I stepped out of the front door heading to my ruby red 2015 Mercedes Benz C-Class with the peanut butter leather interior. Lord knows that car was *everything* and when Marcus surprised me at my 40th birthday party last month, I fell in love all over again. I had been wanting a Mercedes for as long as I could remember, even as a little girl. Marcus knew that and always promised me that once he was able to save enough money from his business, he would make sure I got one.

Marcus was big on not using the money from the church. Unlike a lot of pastors these days, he didn't solely depend on that money to take care of his family. So he started a very lucrative publishing company where he gave Christian Fiction authors who didn't want to follow the norm of Christian writing, an outlet to be able to use the gift that God gave each of them. To date he had six National Bestsellers, himself and ten other authors who all have at least one bestseller a piece.

I'm so proud of that man and love him with all that God has put in me. I had made a decision after everyone left out this morning and while I got dressed that while on this vacation, I would finally have time to sit down and tell Marcus everything that I tried to keep buried deep in the back of my mind. I couldn't go on like this and I just hoped that nothing happened to cause me not to be the one to tell him.

I set the alarm before locking the door and heading out for the day. The weather was a nice breezy 73 degrees and the sun was shining bright. It was Monday also known as my "balance day". Don't get me wrong, I love the Lord with all that's in me but I also believed that God intended for us to enjoy life; therefore, this was my one day of the week to just kick back and not feel like I was sitting on the front row of my mother's old Baptist church having the life sucked out of me.

Quite a few of the seasoned members in the church thought that Marcus and I should follow the same rules that other pastors and first ladies did by always quoting scriptures, laying hands, saying a whole lot of "thou's" and "thus this and that." But when we had the "rule book" that "they" wrote then maybe we would reconsider. Until then, we are gonna teach our children how to love God with their whole hearts, learn His word, and be well rounded individuals.

Now, my ripped stonewashed jeans from my favorite store Torrid, white Michael Kors tee, and fresh out the box retro Jordan 11's didn't scream "First Lady" but contrary to what people believed, I'm not a title, but a person. The day people stopped placing others who were in the church on those high pedestals the world might be a little bit better. Chile I had always been one to rock some jeans and J's over a dress and stilettos anyway. That's just who I was.

I threw my MK tote on the passenger seat, placed my shades on my face, and fastened the seatbelt. I eased out of my driveway with my windows down and my hair blowing in the wind listening to one of my favorite albums on my iPod. Fantasia's "Side Effects of You" flowed through the speakers and until I made it completely out of my neighborhood, I couldn't blast it like I really wanted to. Not because I didn't want anyone calling me a hypocrite, but because those fines the Homeowners Association charged for breaking the noise ordinance were not pretty.

As soon as I got to the main road I hit that volume button on the steering wheel and it was on!

"I'm not scared if I bleed. If I tear it proves to me

The love I shared was worth every drop, drop, drop, drop

And Lord know I don't want this to stop

I wanna go in deep with you

I wanna go in deep with you

I wanna feel your scars and cherish every flaw

I wanna go in deep with you."

I was in my zone singing along with Tasia. Before I could get to the second verse my phone started ringing. Glancing over at the display on my dash I was confused by the "312" Chicago area code looking back at me.

Hitting the hands free button, I hesitantly answered the call. I would normally send calls that were unfamiliar to me straight to voicemail but something told me this was one I needed to take now. I thank God that I was stopped at a red light cause had I not been, I might have crashed into something or someone as soon as I heard the voice on the line.

"Heeeyyyyyy Ronni," the voice said, immediately causing my eyes to water.

"How did you get this number?" I asked driving off slowly towards downtown. I knew the quivering in my voice was very noticeable and there was absolutely no way I could hide it.

"Oh baby you sound so nervous. Do I still have that effect on you after all of these years?"

Ignoring the question I asked, "What do you want?"

"You looked nice this morning when you got in the car. Still fresh to *death* I see." Something about the way the word death was said and the fact that I was being watched caused a chill to run down my spine. And the fact it was at my home made it ten times worse. I had to pull over into the parking lot of the Race Track gas station in order to get my thoughts together.

"How do you know what I looked like this morning, and more importantly where I live?" By now I was livid!

"Awww Ronni, baby you know I have my ways. I always have my ways," the caller said slowly before continuing. "It was nice seeing you at church."

At that moment my blood felt like it was beginning to run cold. It was as if it was snowing outside instead of the sun shining bright as I thought back to yesterday. God knows I had tried so hard not to live in my past and forget about it but now it looked as if it was going to be impossible.

"How did you find me and why after all of these years?" I asked as I got myself together enough to drive down the block and pull into the parking lot of the bank. I had to make sure I deposited the money from the church's collection by a certain time in order for it to post as normal. If the deposit didn't post by a certain time then Marcus would get a notification of the issue.

The last thing I needed was for him to be calling trying to find me before I had my thoughts together. I had to come up with a way to talk to him on my own terms. I prayed that God gave me the right words to say to him.

"Now you didn't think services that your church televised nationally and worldwide on the net would somehow make it hard to find you, did you?"

At that moment I wanted to curse and kick myself for coming up with that idea and bringing it to the board members of the church. Marcus thought it had been such a great idea to be able to reach as many of God's people as possible through those outlets. Had I known it would not only call out the saints but the demons too, I would have kept my mouth shut.

"Well baby girl I know that you have errands to run before Bible study tonight so I will let you go. We will talk soon."

Before I could find the words to say or just hang up I heard, "I wonder how Marcus and God's people will feel towards you when your secrets come out."

"What makes you think my husband doesn't know about my past already? We have no secrets in our marriage," I said trying to sound convincing but failing miserably.

"You can't be serious?" they said laughing like Kevin Hart had just told the funniest joke of his career. Just as soon as the laughter began it stopped. "Had you already told your *wonderful man of God* about us you wouldn't have been so scared when you saw me. Man the look on your face and your legs going weak told on you. It also let me know I still have that effect on you; I could always make you weak with just one look. That's okay baby, we will sit down together with Marcus soon enough and tell him. Have a good day baby girl." And with that the call ended.

For the next twenty minutes all I could do was sit in my car, crying my eyes out and praying to God like never before. I don't know how I thought none of this would ever come back to haunt me. I didn't know which way was up right now cause if my life before I met Marcus came out before I was ready to tell him, it could be all bad. Real bad.

I had no clue what to do but to call on Jesus. He was the only one that would be able to deliver me from this mess. All of these years I thought He had forgiven me but from the looks of it I wasn't too sure of anything right now. All I could keep thinking was this was bad. Real, real bad. God *please* help us all.

Chapter Six

Marcus had already called twice to check on me because I was never late for a counseling session so I knew he was worried. I did my best to assure him I was on my way and that there was a long line at the bank when I went to make the deposit. I tried my best to never lie to him but lately I found myself torn between the truth and the lie. It was just this thing had me so afraid that I couldn't think straight.

Walking into the front of the church, I walked right past Deacon Harper without speaking. Even when he called out to me to get my attention I kept going headed straight to the office used for the counseling sessions. As soon as I walked in I knew I had to take my shades off but right now it felt like those frames were the only protection to my soul that I had. I knew the moment I looked into my husband's eyes he would see my dirty, no good, trifling spirit.

Taking them off I turned my head to the couple before me and gave a half smile to Stephanie and Blake who sat on the love seat together. They sat looking like they had the weight of the world on their shoulders. I could relate because that's exactly how I felt at this very moment.

"Hi First Lady. How are you today?" asked Stephanie giving me a warm smile.

Mustering up the little bit of energy to create a bigger smile of my own I replied, “Hi sweetie. I’m sorry I’m late. That bank was packed today.” All I could hear was the voice of Tamar Braxton when she would holler out “LIES!”

“Oh that’s okay, we understand. We don’t have anything else planned for the day so we are not in a hurry,” Blake replied.

Marcus cleared his throat and said, “Would you two please excuse us a moment before we start? I just need to make sure my wife and I have all of our notes and everything so that we can help the two of you as much as possible.”

“Sure, go ahead, we have time,” Blake said. He was ready to get this session going but he knew that by the look on both his Pastor and First Lady’s faces, they needed a minute.

I knew this was about to happen. I knew my husband and he definitely knew me. I don’t know why I thought a fake smile would have worked. There was no God in that smile and that was not how I rolled. But as much as I wanted to confide in my husband, that moment just wasn't right. I needed to be away from everyone and everything so that I could have his undivided attention. This was heavy and I needed to prepare mentally for what his response would be.

I stepped out into the hallway first and led the way to my office. Once we were inside and the door was closed Marcus just stood there watching me. I never knew how much it bothered me until that very moment, how he would study me. Maybe because it was never anything I had to hide from him, but right now I felt like he was giving me a good read.

Not sure where to start or what to say, I could tell he was at a loss so he asked me, "Baby do we need to reschedule this? I can see there is something terribly wrong. You know that you are my first priority outside of God. I'm sure Blake and Steph would understand."

"No. No I'm okay. I'm just a little tired. Maybe coming down with one of those summer colds or allergies starting to act up. I can do this," I said lying through my glossy Mac covered lips. I was trying like heck to convince myself even more than my husband.

Marcus walked over to me and put his arms around my waist pulling me close. There was no place that I felt safer than in his arms. The love and power that resided in this man was as if I was standing right in the arms of God himself. Man I loved this feeling and wished that I could stay here forever. Nothing was said between us for almost five minutes, but I could feel the strength that I needed coming back to me. He squeezed me a little tighter and told me, "Baby whatever it is that you are facing I'll face it with you. You know that right?"

"Yes baby, I know. Let's go keep a marriage together," I said as I looked up and smiled at him. He led us into a quick prayer that everything we said to Stephanie and Blake was from God. Never did we ever want to give any advice or guidance that wasn't from the

Holy Spirit. I wasn't too sure on praying to or hearing from God right about now but I had to still have faith. In order to do what we set out to do, we had to remove ourselves and let Him speak through us.

Walking back down the hallway to the other office I gave Deacon Harper my signature warm smile. "Good morning Deacon. How are you today?"

By the look on his face I knew he was stunned at my sudden change, but realizing that something deep had to be occupying my mind earlier he returned the smile and said, "I'm fine Lady Veronica. You have a blessed day, you hear? God is still in control."

"That He is," I said as he turned back to his work.

Once we were out of earshot, I didn't know it right then but Deacon Harper went before the Father in prayer for us.

"Lord, I don't know all but I do know you. I know that you will not let your servants fail nor fall. Give them the understanding and the peace that is needed right now

God, and block this attack that the enemy is trying to hit them with. Hold them together when the opinions of the people come against them, cause they are coming Lord, and it will be hard. Give them the strength to stand strong together. Let Pastor's love for his wife, children, and most of all you, never falter nor waver. God, what you put together, let no man or demon put asunder. Have your holy way in your son Jesus name, I pray, Amen. Mmph, this is gonna be a fight right here," he concluded as he went back to washing the front windows of the church.

****

Back in the office with more determination than ever to help this young couple, Marcus and I read over the questionnaire that each one had filled out. The biggest and most important issue that they seemed to be facing was intimacy. That wasn't something that we were personally familiar with because from the moment we met we have had intimate moments. But I did understand not everyone could relate to us. Since we counseled most of the couples in our ministry we knew this was something that was common. Either one was in the mood and the other not so much, or it took one longer to get there than the other spouse. Whatever the reason or situation we were going to give them what God gave to us.

By the time that first session was over, the both of them seemed to be a little more at ease and relaxed than when they first came in. Marcus told them that we would hold at least four more sessions and if they felt they needed more or less to let us know at any time. We were here for them.

We walked them up front to schedule their next session with our liaison Jonah, but before we even made it to her desk, the smell of fresh lilies hit my nose and I couldn't get my feet to move any more.

"Oh hey Pastor and First Lady. These flowers were just delivered to you, Lady Millhouse about ten minutes ago. I was going to ask you if you wanted me to send the person a "thank you" card but there wasn't a card with a name," Jonah said looking in my direction. I couldn't take my eyes off of the flowers though. I can remember in horticulture class when we were going over the different meanings of flowers and lilies were said to be the ones that represented death. From that day on, for some reason they always scared me. About twenty years ago someone gave them to me as a gift and when I explained my fear, they promised to never give them to me again, until today. I knew who sent them and I wanted them out of my sight like yesterday!

"Throw them away," I said as calmly as I could. I saw the looks that everyone gave me but I didn't care; obviously neither did the sender.

Since no one heard me the first time and were standing there with these dumb looks on their faces I repeated myself a little louder this time.

"I SAID THROW THEM AWAY, NOW!" And with that I left them standing there, went to my office to retrieve my purse and keys, and headed to the front door.

"Ronnie, wait!" Marcus said calling me by my nickname and running up behind me. I wasn't trying to hear him right now but I would never flat out disrespect him, especially out in public. The first time someone sees me do that they will stop respecting him and his position.

"Babe listen," he started, "go home and get into your relaxed clothes. I'll clear our schedules for today and get Minister Rockmore to do Bible study. Want me to pick up lunch for us?"

This is exactly why I loved this man. He would do whatever possible to get to the bottom of things and he wouldn't cause a scene. He knew there was something personal going on and I guess that this was finally my opportunity to get things out in the open.

"Okay," I sighed. "Whatever you bring is fine. I don't have an appetite right now, but maybe later. I love you." Kissing him, I walked out and headed to my car. Once I got in and out of the parking lot that same Chicago number displayed once again.

I was not in the mood to keep playing these games. "HELLO!" I yelled. I had to hurry up and tell Marcus because the feeling I had told me if I didn't do it today, I wouldn't have the chance to.

"Awww boo, what's wrong? Didn't you like the beautiful flowers I sent you?"

"You know damn well I didn't! You know I hate those flowers, but right now I think I hate you way more," I said unable to keep my emotions from spilling over.

"Oh my God! Did the First Lady just curse? Sounds like my old boo is coming back," they said as laughter filled the space in the car.

I found nothing remotely funny about what was going on so I had to get to the real reason this was all happening.

"What do you want? I mean why are you coming back after all these years? Is it money?" I asked hoping that would solve the problem. It usually did with people like this.

Once again the laughter stopped abruptly. "Money? Don't you ever insult me like that." I should have known this conversation was about to take a turn for the worse.

"Getting *saved* as you church folks call it, must have caused you to lose your memory, Veronica! Last time I checked I was the one taking care of you! You were a nobody when I met you. *I* upgraded you! So don't you ever fix your mouth to ever insult me like that."

"I didn't mean it like that," I said trying to sound calmer than I felt right now. My hands were shaking and sweating so bad that they were slipping off of the steering wheel.

"I know you didn't baby. I'm sorry I yelled at you. It's just so hard seeing you knowing that I can't touch you like I want to. But to answer your question, I want you."

"Well you know that can't happen. I have a husband and children now. I'm no longer available. And if I were, you would be the last person on the face of the earth that I would want to be with." I wish I could have taken back that last sentence but it was too late.

"Hmph. Oh really?" the tone in their voice chilled me to my bone causing me to stutter through my next few words.

"I-I-I-I I didn't mean to sound harsh," I said trying to sound as sympathetic as I could.

"So not only are you a cursing first lady, but you are a lying first lady, too? I'm not sure your flock would like that."

"That is not who I am and you know it. I didn't mean to sound harsh but I meant what I said, just not how it came out." This cat and mouse, back and forth game was starting to wear on me and it had only been a little over twenty four hours since my past walked back into my life.

Had I been focused on the road more than this telephone call from hell, I would have been able to prevent going through the red light and causing the large utility truck to smash into the side of my car.

But it was too late.

Chapter Seven

Marcus

If it wasn't one thing it was another and it felt like as of recently I didn't know which way was up. Being a pastor of a mega church wasn't easy by a long shot, but I understood that being the wife of a pastor could be harder sometimes. Veronica handled a lot of the day-to-day things for me and if I had to go out of town on a speaking engagement, she would be the one to make sure I had everything I needed, the kids were taken care of, and the church continued to run smooth.

I don't know if I would be able to handle if anything happened to her. Just as soon as that thought crossed my mind as I was headed out of the church, my cell rang.

"Morning, Malachi. What's going on bro?" I said realizing it was Lailani's father calling.

"Hey there, Marcus. I'm hanging in here," he said sounding weary.

"What's wrong? You don't sound too good. Everything alright?"

"I don't think so. I'm here in the ER with Lay Lay and I just saw the EMT rush First Lady to the back. When I tried to find out for sure and get some information, they told me I couldn't get any until family was reached. So I called you right away to see if you had heard anything."

"Where are you?" I asked. Well more like I yelled but not meaning to. All I knew was that I had to get to my wife.

"Piedmont," he said.

"I'm on my way," I said as I got into the car and bailed out. All the way to the hospital I prayed as much as the words would form for me to get out. I couldn't think straight so I know I had to let the Holy Spirit take over that prayer for me.

I got to Piedmont Hospital in record time and I just barely parked before I was jumping out of the car, running into the emergency room doors. I felt like I was reliving the day that Veronica went into labor with MJ all over again, but this was a totally different emotion I was feeling. Instead of excitement and joy I was feeling scared and nervous.

Before I could find a nurse to tell me what was going on I heard Malachi call my name from the door that led to the back. I got to him as fast as I could to find out what was going on.

"Here is your pass. I told them I was one of your ministers in training at church and that you were on the way. She's in room twenty eight. Torre and I won't leave until we find out what's going on. We're still waiting on test results for Lay."

"Thanks buddy. When I find out what's going on. I'll be back to check on Lailani. What room is she in?" I asked. Although I was in a hurry and worried about Veronica I still wanted them to know I would be there for them as well.

"She's in room sixteen. Come when you can but take care of Veronica first," he said walking down the hall with me.

"Will do," I said as I followed the signs to my wife's room. Once I got outside of the door I didn't know what to expect, so I braced myself as I knocked lightly and walked in.

The sight before me was one to almost bring me to my knees. The doctor that was inside checking Veronica's vitals had to stop what he was doing in order to catch me.

"Whoa there! Come on I got you buddy," he said as he helped me to the chair at the foot of her bed. "You must be Mr. Millhouse?"

"Yes. What happened to my wife? She had only been gone about ten minutes," I asked not able to wrap my mind around what was really going on.

"Well from the report I got from the EMT's, a utility truck hit her on the passenger side when she ran through a red light. The police have a little more info than I do. I can get them if you'd like."

"Is she going to be ok?" I ignored the statement about the police. I wasn't trying to deal with them until I found out how my wife would be.

"Well she is one blessed lady. Her injuries could have been a lot worse if the impact was done from the driver's side. The injuries she did sustain are relatively minor in comparison to some," the doctor was saying. I didn't understand why doctors always went around the burning bush thirty five times before just answering a question; must have been what they were taught in medical school.

"She suffered a slight concussion when the truck pushed her into a light pole on the driver's side, and the impact also caused her left arm and leg to get slightly crushed against it. She suffered a hairline fracture to her left hip, and lots of bruising and scarring on her body, but she will make a full recovery. Her vitals are good and we gave her something for the pain so she may be out for a while."

Although my baby looked worse on the outside than she really was I was just glad to know that she would be okay.

"Thanks doc. If the police are outside you can send them on in so I can send them on their way after they ask all of these questions," I told him. He shook my hand and let me know if there was anything we needed to let him or one of the nurses know.

Before I had time to get up and go over to Veronica's bed, one uniformed officer and two detectives came into the room.

"Mr. Millhouse?" the short white detective asked. I could already tell that he had a chip on his shoulder by the way he carried himself.

"Pastor Millhouse. Do you know what happened to my wife?" I asked. I was not in the mood to be played with while my wife was laid up in a hospital bed.

"Hello Pastor. I'm Detective Benny Ramos and this is my partner Detective Patrick Johansen," said the taller of the two men. His spirit lined up with mine better than that other one so I could deal with him right now.

"Nice to meet you, Detective," I said shaking his hand.

"Officer Norman was the first officer on the scene and he can give you much of the details before your wife was transferred to the hospital," Detective Ramos said giving the officer the floor.

"The few witnesses that were there including the utility truck driver stated that your wife seemed to be distracted," Officer Norman said. She looked familiar and I realized she had visited the church a few times with one of the mothers of the church, and either her husband or boyfriend.

"She was probably texting or doing something illegal," said Detective Johansen. He was on a thin line and needed to watch himself. I felt the old Marcus coming out and that was definitely not a good look.

"No one said that she was texting. They said that she looked to be in a heated argument and that caused her not to be fully aware of her surroundings," Officer Norman finished.

"So was it you that she was arguing with? Were the two of you having a marital dispute?"Johansen smirked when he said that.

Instead of allowing me to answer the question like my flesh wanted me to, the Lord allowed Detective Ramos to intervene.

"Is your number uh '312-555-6341'?" he asked me.

"No. I have a '678' area code, why?" I asked confused as to why he was asking me about a Chicago phone number.

"This was the last number that your wife received a call from right before the accident. I'm thinking if we can get in touch with the caller we might be able to find out what happened right before the collision."

"Did you guys already try to call the number?" I asked wondering why they hadn't been able to speak with the person already.

"Well we tried to place a call to it and discovered it was one of those burner or disposable type cell phones. We noticed there were only two calls from that number in your wife's call log," Officer Norman informed me.

"And neither call was outgoing. They were both incoming calls," Detective Ramos immediately confirmed. I guess by the look on my face he knew that question was coming next and he wanted to ease my mind.

"Other than that, we don't have too much more information. The utility worker is cooperative and very remorseful. He tried to stop the impact but by the truck being so large he couldn't get it to stop right away."

"I understand. I know those trucks can't just stop like a car might be able to. I'm sure he didn't mean for it to happen. No charges will be filed will they?" I said knowing the driver was probably just as shaken up as everyone else.

"Only if you want them to be." Johansen was working on everybody's nerves by now. I'm not sure how his partner was able to even work with him on a daily basis.

"No, it wasn't his fault," I heard come from behind me. I turned around to see my baby's eyes open then shut right away. The light may have been too bright for her, but God knows I was thankful she could even open them as I rushed to her side.

Chapter Eight

Veronica

"Beep...Beep....Beep....Beep," was the noise I heard above my head before I heard the voices. It took me a minute to gather my thoughts but then I realized one of the voices was that of Marcus. I didn't know how long I had been here but I was glad I wasn't alone.

I knew the conversation was about the accident that I was now remembering. So when I heard the question being asked to charge the utility worker, I had to speak up.

"No, it wasn't his fault," I said as I slowly opened my eyes, but quickly closed them once again. That light above me was too bright right now. But I was able to get a quick peek at my husband and saw the relief wash over his handsome face.

"Hey babe," he said rushing over to my side. He gently placed a kiss on my lips and held the hand that wasn't bandaged up. "Are you okay, Ronnie?" I hated to see worry lines on his forehead but as long as I could see him I would deal with them.

"Really sore but I'm okay. Is anything broken? Why am I all bandaged up?" I asked noticing my arm in a sling, but from my left hip down it looked like a cast. Marcus informed me of everything he was told and any questions he didn't know the answers to, the nice officer and detective filled us both in. That little short fat one did something to me though. I didn't like his spirit too much. I knew I John, chapter four, verse one said,

"Beloved, do not believe every spirit, but test the spirits to see whether they are from God, for many false prophets have gone out into the world."

A lot of people thought it was how "church folk" just got away with judging people when they really didn't understand. Those feelings that you get when you are around someone and something in you doesn't feel right, that's the Holy Spirit letting you know to keep your eyes open. Not all the time will it be something bad but God is alerting us to be mindful of whom we are around.

Now granted, some do use that as a form of judgment thinking they are lining up with God's word but they are only making that fit how they want it to fit and not like God intended. That's a dangerous thing to do but not every believer is like that.

So what my spirit was saying right now was to just watch this detective. Not to give him this nasty attitude, but to make sure to keep an eye on him. I knew Marcus was feeling the same way I was about him.

Once they finished getting the information they needed, Officer Norman gave us her card and wished me well, as did Detective Johansen. They both let us know that if we thought of anything or needed them to feel free to give them a call. We thanked them and they were on their way.

As soon as the door closed Marcus pulled up a chair beside the bed and sat there rubbing my hand. He saw the pain that I was going through by the look on my face when I tried to turn my body.

"The doctor said you would be in a lot of pain for a while but you will make a full recovery. But for now I want you as comfortable as possible," he said pressing the nurse call button on the bed railing.

"How can I help you?" said the nurse on the intercom.

“My wife is in severe pain and needs something for it, please,” he said to her.

“Of course, sir, I’ll be right in with her next dosage.”

“Thank you,” he said before the call light went out.

There was a knock at the door and we assumed it was the nurse coming in. As soon as she entered to take my vitals before giving me my medicine there was another knock. Marcus got up to open the door and welcomed Malachi, Torre, and Lailani into the room.

I assumed by the looks on their faces that they were worried about me. I didn’t know they were there for any other reason. I got up the best smile I could as the nurse was starting to give me the morphine and I said, “Why the long faces? I’ll be fine y’all.”

I swear this medicine had to be making me hear things because I could have sworn I heard Lailani’s mother Torre say, “Lay’s pregnant,” before the drug took me under.

Chapter Nine

Marcus

If there were any moment in my life that I wished I was deaf, this would be the time. Veronica was lucky the medicine took her under but I was left to figure out what was going on. So many thoughts were running through my mind and I had no clue where to begin.

I stood there for another minute or so fighting to get the words I was thinking to come out of my mouth, but the struggle was real.

"Say what now?" I finally asked.

I looked from Malachi to Torre to Lailani and I could tell they were all in their own worlds, but I needed for them to come back to this one.

"Who's the father?" I asked and that got their attention. If looks could kill I would be gone right now by the way they were all looking at me. "Listen, I know that may sound messed up but you can't blame me for asking. I have to know so that I can know how to deal with this accordingly."

I guess they thought about the situation and understood where I stood. If the roles were reversed they would be asking me the same thing.

"We understand Marcus. This is a lot to deal with especially with first lady being in the accident. How is she anyway? What happened?" said Torre. Lailani was still standing there with tears falling down her face as I walked over to give her a comforting hug.

I explained all that I knew up until this point about what happened to Veronica and even after saying it out loud again I was more confused than ever. Things just weren't adding up. I started to wonder if this had anything to do with why she had been so stressed and if it was weighing on her. I never knew she had any ties to anyone in Chicago so this was a first for me.

I put my focus back on the new revelation and asked, "How far along?"

"Thirteen weeks. They have been hiding this for all of this time. Both her and MJ already knew," Malachi said.

"What? That's around what, three months?" I asked looking down at Lailani's stomach. Now that the cat was out of the bag I could definitely see her belly protruding. I don't know how any of us had missed this because it was so obvious.

"From our understanding it happened the night Malachi and I went out for our anniversary dinner. She was supposed to be at home with her best friend Jamie and Jamie's cousin for the night but they ended up sneaking in MJ, Jacobi, and some other boy," Torre said.

"Wait a minute," I said as I thought back to their anniversary weekend. It was clear now because Veronica and I were supposed to join them but her sinuses started bothering her and we couldn't go.

"I remember that night. After we canceled with you guys MJ asked if he could spend the night with Cobi. How did I not see something was up? He never asks to spend the night over there. The only reason we said okay was so the house would be quiet and she could rest. The girls were already at a sleepover," I said shaking my head.

"Don't beat yourself up about this. None of us knew what was going on right under our noses. I can't believe this happened," said Malachi walking towards the window.

"This is what we will do. Once I get Ronnie home and she's settled, y'all come over to the house so we can all sit down and discuss this together."

“Okay. Just let us know what time to be there. If Veronica isn’t up for it today we can get together maybe tomorrow or Wednesday.”

We agreed on the time and they headed out to leave. I couldn’t believe this was happening but I needed God more than ever during this moment. I knew once the congregation found out we would have to do damage control. Hopefully it wouldn’t be too bad but I knew it would be uncomfortable. I also had to pray that neither I nor Veronica would do any harm to MJ.

We tried so hard to raise our children right and thought that we were doing a good job for them. This was definitely a curveball the devil has thrown but I knew God was the umpire and He was the one to make the final call.

****

I could tell Veronica was still out of it because all the way home she was in and out of sleep. Even as I stopped by the drug store to get her prescriptions filled, she slept. The doctor told her to be on bed rest for the next two weeks, so there goes our family vacation. I really wasn't in the mood to go away right now anyway; not with Ronnie getting hurt, the news that I'm about to be a grandfather, and still not knowing what was going on with Veronica... the trip would be everything but fun and relaxing. I needed to know what was going on with her but there is something in me saying it wasn't going to be easy to hear. We had never been the ones to keep anything from each other no matter how big of a pill it was to swallow, so her behavior had me puzzled.

As we were pulling into the driveway I was glad to see the kids getting off of the bus. I was going to need help getting their mother's things out while I took her in the house. I also wanted to get a chance to talk to MJ before she woke up and remembered what she heard.

"Oh my God, what happened to mommy? Is she alright?" Dynasty asked with them all running up to us.

"She's fine now. She was in a car accident but the Lord protected her. Help me get her stuff out of the car while I take her inside."

They all nodded their heads and did as I asked of them. They knew I would need them to help out a little bit more around the house and I'm glad that they were willing.

As soon as I got Veronica inside our master suite, I tried to help her get comfortable as much as I could. I got her out of those scrubs that were provided for her since her own clothes were destroyed by the EMTs, and changed her into her favorite Georgia Bulldogs t-shirt. Just as I was about to leave out of the room and find out where MJ was, she woke up.

"Babe?" she said just above a whisper. I ran back over to her side to make sure she was okay.

"I'm here baby. I'm right here," I said doing an awful job of hiding my anxiety. The last thing I wanted her to do was worry. We needed for her to have a full recovery.

"My mouth is dry. Can I get something to drink please?" she asked. I hated to see her in this condition. My life partner was out of commission for a while and I didn't know how to adjust just yet. Eventually I knew I would but right now I was torn.

I had one of the twins bring her some water and got ready to get her next dose of medicine. Doctor Harper said it was best to make sure I give it to her on the right schedule so that when it's time to stop taking them she won't be in nearly as much pain.

"Here you go mommy," Destiny said as she came in the room with the water. She eased down beside her mother doing her best not to create too much motion on the bed. I propped Veronica up slightly as I placed the pills in her mouth and Dez helped her drink from the straw.

She must have been really thirsty because she took that whole glass down in a matter of seconds.

Laying her back down on the pillows as gently as possible, I watched her struggle to get comfortable. Once she did she said,

"Des, thank you princess. You can go ahead and get your homework started."

"You sure mommy?" she asked reluctantly. Out of all of the children, Destiny was the most attached to her mother. Not saying the other two weren't, but for as long as I could remember Destiny would spend all of her free time up under her mother when she could.

"Yea baby, I'm fine. Go ahead and get started then come back and check on me in a little bit, okay?" she asked as she smiled at her. Even in her condition she made sure to still put a smile on her face and comfort someone else. *God how I loved this woman*.

Destiny gave her a quick peck on the cheek and headed to her room like she was told. I knew Veronica and I had to talk but I wasn't sure which subject to speak on and if this was the best time. She needed her rest first.

"So what do you want to talk about first?" she asked. I swear sometimes I thought she was a mind reader.

"Do you think we should do this now? You need your rest baby."

"Quit stalling. I know what I need but I also know what *we* need as well," she said making her finger go in a circling motion to include us and the kids.

Continuing she said, "Remember our first ministry is home. Nothing comes before that. If home is not right there is no way we can effectively minister to others."

I knew she was right but I guess I was just worried about how everything was going to play out. It was true that every once in a while no matter how far we are in our walk with the Lord, there were still some days and situations that got to us more than others. I wouldn't be keeping it real if I said with being a pastor, I had everything together.

"I need to know how you are before we deal with MJ. I need you to be free of whatever it is that has been sent to attack you," I said. She took a deep breath, reached for my hand and began to pray.

Chapter Ten

Veronica

As I lay here looking at Marcus I can't tell what's going on in his mind. Is he mad at me? Is he disgusted with me? Does he even want to stay married to me? All of these things were going through my mind at the same time. Before either of us could say anything there was a knock on our bedroom door.

"Come in," said Marcus as MJ opened the door and walked in.

"I just wanted to check on mom and see if you guys needed anything before I asked to go over to Lay's house.

She said she needed to talk to me," he said, obviously in the dark so far about us knowing his secret.

I looked over at Marcus and I could see the flames coming from his ears as he watched our son stand there so calm. I gently placed my hand on the lower part of his back and rubbed it slowly. I often did this to calm him down when I knew he was about to go from zero to a hundred real quick.

I felt the tension leave his body so I knew it was working as he told MJ to have a seat on the bed. I tried to get into a different position but as soon as I moved I felt like I was being hit by the truck again.

"JESUS!" I screamed.

"Baby, you okay? What's wrong? Do we need to go back to the hospital?" Marcus asked me, jumping up.

"Mom, are you alright? Was it me?" MJ asked with his face full of fear and his eyes watering.

The twins also ran into the room to check on me. The pain was so unbearable that it took me a few seconds to even nod my head to let them know I was alright. This medicine needed to kick in fast.

"I'm okay, I'm okay. I just moved the wrong way. It's not your fault baby," I said to MJ. The sad look in his eyes almost made me feel sorry for him and his situation. I said almost.

The pain finally eased up and I could feel the meds beginning to take effect. If we didn't get this show on the road I was about to be out once again, probably until the next morning and it was only 4pm.

"Well since all of you are in here I think that we should go ahead and discuss this as a family," Marcus started.

"Daddy you don't have to explain the family vacation. We know we can't go and we understand. Making sure mommy is okay is our only focus," Destiny said speaking for her and her siblings. Dynasty and MJ both nodded their heads in agreement. That was why we loved our children so much; they were so unselfish and thought about the well being of other people first.

"I'm glad you all are understanding about that. Hopefully we can still go before the summer is over and mommy is feeling much better," Marcus said. "But we have a bigger issue to talk about right now," he said looking over at MJ. Now either MJ was a good actor or he really thought we didn't know about Lailani being pregnant.

"What I do?" he asked looking back between us all. By the looks on the twin's faces they were in the dark as well. If Destiny knew about a secret she would have already told by now. She couldn't hold water in a cup. And if Dynasty knew a secret, she would keep it hidden but her face would be a dead giveaway in our presence.

"Is there anything that you need to tell us son?" I asked. Hopefully he would get the hint and just say it but right now he was holding on to this for dear life.

"Malachi was the one who called to let me know your mother was in the hospital. He saw her come in while he and Torre were there with Lailani," Marcus was explaining while I watched the reactions of all of the kids, especially MJ. So far they all looked confused and wanted to know where this was going.

Marcus paused to see if anyone would step in. I hated when it took him forever to get to the bottom line. Since no one said anything, he continued.

"Once they finished with Lailani they came over to see how Ronnie was doing and they shared something with us." Now the color looked like it was starting to drain from Mj's face like dish water drained from the sink. He looked like he was about to release everything he had in his stomach for the last couple of days. It served him right though. He should have never put himself or Lailani in this situation, but we would do our best to work through this.

"Is Lailani okay daddy?" Dynasty asked. Although the twins were younger than Lailani they loved her like a big sister and were pretty close, so for them not to know what was going on shocked both Marcus and myself.

"She's fine. She's three months pregnant," I said dropping the bomb as Destiny and Dynasty's eyes got big as saucers and MJ allowed the tears to fall. I wanted to tell him, "Naw buddy, too late for those tears!" but I had to have a different approach if we wanted a positive outcome. He didn't need us to kick him while he was down. Although he is the one who made the decision to have unprotected sex, we knew we needed to be there for our child. He was going to have a time being a teen father.

"Wait, what?" Dynasty asked. I hated when she said 'what' like that although she thought it was the funniest thing ever. Destiny elbowed her in the side to remind her that this wasn't a laughing matter.

"Well?" Marcus asked MJ.

"I'm so sorry dad. I know we were wrong but I won't continue to lie and tell you that I didn't enjoy it."

"Girls go to your room!" Marcus and I both said at the same time. It just got real. If I was mobile, MJ would be immobile after I came across that head. See now all that other logic done went out the window cause now he thinking because he done got him a little sniff, he was grown. Let me bring that behind back, real quick like.

Before I could say or do anything Marcus was in his face.

"Let me tell you something son," he started calmly. When Marcus talked through gritted teeth and those words came out real calm that was the Lord trying to help him stay saved. If he got to yelling, it was a wrap. I needed God to intervene and keep the situation under control cause if MJ got grown and they got to tussling and broke anything in my room, they both needed to worry about me digging off in those behinds. Besides that's not how we should handle things, but just because we live our life after God's own heart doesn't mean we're all the way delivered yet.

Coming back from my side tracked thought, I focused back in to see Marcus holding on to his son as MJ broke down crying in his arms. I don't even know what Marcus said to make him break like that. Maybe the meds need to wear off a little so I can stay focused.

"I'm so sorry dad. I messed up big time and now Lailani's life is messed up because of me. I didn't mean to let the temptation get to me. I really didn't. I messed up! I messed up! I messed up!" he sobbed into his father's shoulders. I couldn't help but to feel my child's pain as the liquid prayers began to flow from my eyes.

"Shhh, hush son. We are gonna figure this out. Your mother and I are here for you. This was a mistake. We all make mistakes. We are not proud of when we are young and even as adults we fall." As he said that he was looking me dead in my face.

"But the key is not to stay down. We have to get back up and know when we have a support system that is going to help us through our tough times. You have a strong support system. We love you and we forgive you," he finished. I’m not sure if he was speaking to me about my past or just to our son, but at that moment I felt the most freedom than I had in the last twenty years.

Chapter Eleven

Veronica

About three weeks had passed since the accident and us finding out we were about to be grandparents. As tough as it was to deal with, there was a blessing in knowing that MJ really did have a good girl who came from a good family. We know not everyone is perfect but it gave us comfort to know the relationship between our two families was a really good one.

Although the sling was removed from my arm and I was able to move freely now, I still had the cast on my leg. If all went well at my next appointment in two weeks that would be coming off, too. Marcus had taken some time off from the church. We had an awesome staff and friends that God put in our lives. We knew that they all would be able to handle the church functions in our absence.

Marcus would drop by every few days just to check on them and see if they needed anything while he ran errands. Thank goodness we were able to stream Sunday services and Wednesday night Bible study. A few times I told Marcus to go ahead to church, I would be fine; but he was not leaving my side. Deep down I was glad that he stayed with me.

Torre and Malachi would come over to bring by the flowers and cards that were brought to the church for me whenever they got some free time. Lailani was having a really hard time with this pregnancy and being sick day in and day out. We had also found out that during our absence that someone spilled the beans about her being pregnant and that had a lot to do with how she was feeling.

Shame was a powerful demon. It made you feel like everyone was looking at you and judging you and your situation when in reality, half of those people we thought knew our faults really didn't know or even care. But Shame will make us feel that way, and that's how that other demon called Depression would creep in.

All they do is feed off of each other and before you know it, they're having a house party in your spirit along with their friends Guilt, Defeat, Hurt, and the big boss Anger. Their "turn up" would be too real, and if there aren't people around who really love and care for you it could be a hard thing to overcome.

That's why once we all sat down with Lailani and her parents we made sure they knew we had their back. We didn't do that "Momma's baby, Daddy's maybe" mess. We knew our child made that bed and he was going to have to lay in it. Lailani was a really good child and just like any normal teenager she had her ways about her; but being into every dude just wasn't one of them.

That chance we had gotten to just sit and listen to both her and MJ to really see where their heads were at. Listening to them you wouldn't think that they were as young as they are and that was something we all were proud of. As much as we wanted them to try and remain children as long as they could, we had to face the fact that they were growing up.

****

Pulling up to the front of the church I was filled with nothing but joy and excitement. It felt like forever since the last time I was here. Just as Marcus got my chair out of the trunk, one of the members walked up to him.

"Good morning Pastor," he said getting Marcus's attention.

"Oh, good morning, Brother Ron. How have you been?" he asked.

"Blessed and highly favored! God has sho' nuff been good to me," Brother Ron said.

Chuckling a little, Marcus replied, "That's good to hear. It feels good to be able to have my family back in church once again now that Lady Veronica is feeling a little better."

"Yes, yes. Umm Pastor I won't hold you long but I have a quick question."

"Sure what's going on?" he asked placing the chair on the ground and crossing his arms. I watched from the side view mirror of the car, and since the kids were already inside getting my seat together I could hear every word.

"Well there have been a few rumors going on around here that I think you should be aware of."

"Like what?" Marcus asked clearly getting agitated. He had some idea what Ron was about to say but he was hoping he was wrong.

"First there is talk of MJ getting Deacon Malachi's daughter Lailani pregnant."

"That's not a rumor," he simply stated.

If it had been under any other circumstances the expression on Ron's face would have been hilarious. But considering what the subject was it was no laughing matter. Knowing that no one in our family or the Abram's house was ready to disclose that information, it got me to thinking how did people find out so soon. That wasn't the kicker though. What Ron said next kicked me right on over the cliff.

"In addition to that people are saying that First Lady was involved in a-"

"Let me stop you right there Ronald," Marcus interrupted. "First of all I thank you for thinking that you are bringing to my attention the happenings during my absence. But in all reality if there is anyone that knows the goings on in *my* home it's me. My son and Lailani are human and make mistakes as we all do. And they have full support from their family during this time in their lives. Second, my wife's *past* is no one's concern in her *present*. That's what's wrong with a lot of people these days. They love to continue living in someone else's past when the person has already been forgiven by God. You can't get on with your life for constantly being in other's lives. We all have a past. Some worse than other's but it doesn't mean that we should continue to make others feel like they can’t overcome. What I suggest sir, is that the next time anyone comes to you with another person’s business that you mind your own. Enjoy the service.”

Believe me when I say Marcus makes me prouder and prouder each day to be his wife. Now the old me would have cussed him under the table, but I thank God for deliverance from that demon. I would have created a few new curse words for him.

“Ready baby?” he asked me while opening my door.

“Yea. I love you man of God,” I said lovingly.

“I love you more, woman of God,” he said as we headed inside.

Once we got inside it was a mix of emotions and welcome backs. The majority of them were excited to see us back and that I was doing well. But we did notice a few smirks and side eyes as we headed up to the front. Our children were sitting up on the front row as we headed their way and I could see the demeanor in them had changed from about fifteen minutes ago.

"What's the matter?" I asked them looking into each of their faces.

Destiny was the first one to respond with a look of anger displayed across her pretty brown face. It amazed me how much she looked like me when she made certain faces even though she had an identical twin.

"Some of the kids are over in the youth department talking about Lay Lay being pregnant and how MJ's trifling for getting her pregnant."

"Yea talkin' bout only thots get pregnant in high school. Why do people have to be so mean and insensitive?" Destiny said. I could tell MJ was getting more upset by the second but was trying to hold it together.

"I don't understand how it got out. No one was supposed to say anything until we all decided it was the right time," I said.

"I know mom, and none of us said anything. We just got here and heard some kids talking about it and when I stepped to them they wanted to try and back peddle," MJ explained.

"Well the last thing we need is for you to be fighting in church. We are already on people's radars so it looks like we are going to have to tread lightly. Have you seen Lailani and her parents?" Marcus asked. For a second I forgot he was standing behind me.

"I called Mr. Abrams to give him a heads up and he said that they wouldn't be coming today because Lay is sick. Can we go see her after church?" MJ asked.

"Sure. We will find out if they need anything before we go. I bet after this baby you both think long and hard before getting into this situation again," I said.

"I'm done and I'm not even the one carrying it. Just seeing her uncomfortable like this makes me upset."

"I understand son. I've been there twice already so I feel your pain. Let's get situated so we can start service on time then get up out of here," Marcus said as he helped me get into my seat at the front.

Today was our testimony service. We did this about two or three times a year where we would let members of our congregation stand up and give their testimonies. It was always a pleasure to hear the things that God did for others and to give hope to the ones who had doubts that He could bless them too.

Because the church was so big we couldn't possibly get everyone in during one service, so we would have a service that morning and then another that evening. If we still had more testimonies that were untold we made sure to get them to write them down and every time we had a service or function, we would read a few. There was no way that we wanted people to feel left out that they didn't get the opportunity to share.

I knew I probably shouldn't have taken my medicine that morning but the pain was starting to creep back in and I had no choice. Now I was starting to feel sleepy and was fighting to stay awake. The last thing I wanted to happen was that the camera picked up a shot of me falling asleep in church for the world to see. That would be so embarrassing.

We were about an hour into the testimonies. There were people praising God about family members getting saved and set free; some had been praying for jobs and God opened those doors for them. There were even a few people who stood up to acknowledge the fact that they were addicted to certain drugs or habits and wanted God to break them free from those things. It was just an amazing time. We laughed and we cried. We sang and we rejoiced. Then Satan entered.

Anyone familiar with the word of God knows that He tells us in John chapter ten, verse ten that the thief comes only to steal, kill, and destroy. I don't know why I thought today would be any different.

Everyone that wanted to give a testimony was instructed to form lines in the aisles and we would take as many as we could before the service ended at noon. People were moving pretty quickly unless there was a move of God after someone's testimony; then we had to let Him have his way rejoicing.

I was sitting next to one of our members who had just had her baby recently, and she allowed me the pleasure of holding her daughter. It really started to excite me to know there would be another little one running around our house soon. But before I could go further into my thoughts it was time for the next person's testimony. I couldn't have been more excited for each and every one who got up to share.

When God was moving it was the best feeling in the world and although we were dealing with our own issues, we couldn't help but to celebrate with the people God had placed in our lives.

Chapter Twelve

Marcus

"Good morning church, my name is Ieshia McClendon," One of our new members said as she came up to the mic. I knew she had just joined because each time we had them join we made sure to get their picture along with their information so we could put a name with the face. That was something that I learned from visiting another church in Pensacola, Fl and I thought it was such a good idea.

The woman was very beautiful on the outside. Her clothes were nice and her hair and makeup were put together giving her this flawless look. However, there was something that was going on in the inside that to the naked eye you couldn't see, but my spiritual eyes were wide open.

"Good morning," the people replied. Most of the men were ogling and not even trying to hide it while some of the women were trying to hide their disdain for her and failing miserably at it.

"First I want to give honor to God who is the head of my life," she started. Why did everyone always start their speech off like that? Was that somewhere in a "How To Start A Church Speech" manual? The thought of that tickled me as I continued to listen.

"Second I want to congratulate Bishop and First Lady Millhouse on the upcoming birth of their first grandchild by their son, Marcus, Jr. You all may know him as MJ," she said with the biggest fake smile I had ever seen on someone. I was livid by now and when I looked over at Veronica, she looked like she was about to pass out any second from the breath she was holding in. If there was any doubt that the church was whispering already, this was surely the confirmation we got. People were definitely talking and it wasn't looking good.

Everyone was now wearing confused looks on their faces with the new revelation. This was not how we wanted to tell our church. Some may think we don't owe them an explanation and I guess to some degree we don't. But being spiritual leaders to them we still had a responsibility to make sure that everything we did, we held ourselves accountable.

"Well by the looks of it I let the cat out of the bag. I apologize." She called herself apologizing. She knew exactly what she was doing.

"Let me just move on rapidly. I want to tell you that the God I serve is an awesome God, and I'm only standing here today by the grace He has shown me. Years ago I was a mess; young, wild, and living a dangerous lifestyle. But I had a praying mother," Iesha said.

“I know that’s right baby!” a few of the members said along with others, praising God for the prayers and getting her through this rough time. Once everyone started to get quiet again she continued. She needed everyone to hear what she had to say about her “god”.

“The harder she prayed the further I strayed though. I didn’t want to hear about anyone I couldn’t see. Someone that was supposedly all knowing and all seeing and all powerful. I was thinking if he was all of this then why would he allow me to be out here selling my body to men who didn’t love me just to get my next hit. Just as I was starting to completely give up I saw a glimmer of hope, or so I thought.” She paused to wipe the crocodile tears that were beginning to fall as one of the ushers brought her some tissue.

“Bless you,” she said and continued on. “I apologize for crying but this is so hard for me to tell. I have been holding on to this for so long and finally I know this is the time to share it.”

"That's alright. Let Him use yo,." one of the members beside her said.

Iesha smiled at her and looked up to see she had the undivided attention of everyone under the sound of her voice. This power she felt was better than any drug or orgasm she could ever have. To know that everything that was about to unravel in the next few seconds would all be because of the power she held.

"He sent me my savior - the one who was supposed to help me to get better. And it worked for a while. He had sent me my soul mate; the love of my life to take me up out of the situation I was in, but it didn't happen like that. Instead of being in love with me I was treated exactly like the type of person I was - a tramp on the streets. I was sent out to turn tricks every night and never was able to keep any of the money. I had to turn it all in and continue to struggle. Of course by looking at my appearance you wouldn't know this was happening to me because I stayed fly. That was the only way that I could attract the john's that I did.

Who wanted to sleep with an unclean smelly hoe and then have to pay her for her services? None that I know of that's for sure." There were so many looks of disgust and confusion on the members faces that they didn't know if this was a testimony anymore. It was looking more like a bad accident. You didn't want to see it but you couldn't look away from it.

I reached over to Ronnie and took the baby out of her arms and handed the child back to her mother. I knew Veronica hadn't gotten past the revelation of MJ's baby because she was still stuck in that 'deer in headlights' phase. This testimony better be a good one cause right now it felt like God had taken a break from sitting on His throne.

"I'm almost done and then I will get out of you guys way and let someone else come up. But God has just been so good to me! Long story short I fell so deeply in love that it was beginning to scare me but I was finally getting what I was craving... just to be loved. My mother loved me but not the in way I was yearning to be loved. I wanted that old school kind of love; that fairytale kind of romance, and I thought I had found it.

I started to be wined and dined, taken on shopping sprees and buying the things that I was never able to afford; riding around in cars that cost more than some people's yearly salaries. I thought I was living the life. I was so horribly mistaken. I had fallen so deeply in love with my pimp." Iesha paused. This was a performance for her and I could tell she knew how to work a crowd. She had them mesmerized, including me.

"My mother kept telling me that I had to leave this lifestyle yada, yada, yada, and how God was not pleased with what I was doing. Who wanted to hear that your choices were wrong when finally I was feeling at peace. I had moved up from a corner girl to now living in a five thousand square foot condo. God was in the blessing business so I didn't know what my mother was talking about. I was receiving blessings every day. But I had no clue that the devil will bless you too and make it look like it's God. Anyway, for years I became the main girl. I was even recruiting other talent, if you will.

Then one day my world came crashing down. I had just gotten back from visiting my family down south because my aunt was severely ill. When I walked in the house the air was filled full of gospel music. There was luggage sitting down the hall in front of our bedroom. Running down the hall scared of the sight that I would see, I stopped just inches of being able to see inside.

When I did get the nerve to look, I saw the love that I had spent the last year and a half with look up with tears falling and said 'I'm leaving.' I rushed over to the bed crying hysterically and not knowing which way was up. I was so lost and so confused and I blamed myself."

By now those crocodile tears were long gone and the real ones that exposed the hurt from deep down within her poured out. Church should have been over by now but no one wanted to move until she had finished.

"Leave? Why? Is it something I did? Are you upset that I went out of town? I was going to ask your permission but I had to go right away. I'm so sorry I will never leave your side again. Tell me how to fix this," she continued on.

"'I can't live like this anymore. This isn't me. This isn't the life God planned for me. I had time to think while I was here alone and I was finally able to hear the voice of God speak to me. I knew if I didn't give my life over to Him right then, there was no way of escape for me. So I did. I hope you can understand but I needed to get myself right,' she told me," Ieshia said.

"Can you all imagine the foolery I was hearing from the same person who set up tricks for me, sold me to the highest bidder, used drugs like I did, and sexed me down better than anyone I had ever encountered?" she said looking around at the overflowing of people in the church.

By now Iesha's face had changed into something distorted almost and the look in her eyes was now an empty one, void of any life what so ever.

“I sat there begging and begging until I heard the front door close. I cried like a baby that night and even into the next day. My world and my heart were crushed. That was until a few months ago when I saw her for the first time after all of these years. It was like God was giving me another chance... one more chance to make it right and hopefully fall back in line where we left off. I never stopped loving; I couldn’t just turn my feelings off like that, and I was hoping that the feeling was mutual.

I always told God that if I was able to just get one chance to ask what happened I would accept that answer and have closure. He’s allowing me that chance and I thank God for that. So I want to know. I need to know. Veronica, why did you leave me?”

Silence.

Chapter Thirteen

Marcus

Driving home from this church service, or should I say church circus, had to have been one of the longest drives I have ever taken in the forty years I had been on the face of this earth. Embarrassed would be an understatement, but I knew what I was feeling couldn't compare to what Veronica was going through. I glanced over at her in the passenger seat and my heart broke more watching her with her eyes closed and the tears streaming down her face.

I reached over to her and grabbed her hand as I used my thumb to rub the inside of her palm. I always did that when I didn't have any words to comfort her. It was like my way of telling her that I had her back no matter what. Sure people are going to look at me crazy for standing by her, but what else was I supposed to do? I know the woman that I met all those years ago was not the woman who was described in that so called testimony. That may have been her life before me but hasn't been since me.

"I'm so sorry Marcus," she said, barely audible.

"We'll talk about it when we get home. Not right now," I said looking at our children in the back seat. Each one of them had confused expressions on their faces but no one said a thing.

When we finally reached the house Torre and Malachi were sitting in their car with Lailani in the back seat. I couldn't read the expressions on their faces but I already knew why they were there. They weren't at church but I know they were streaming in from home. I just prayed to God no one said anything crazy cause *Pastor* Millhouse would be gone and *Mark* was going to be available.

Getting out of the car we all just looked at each other without saying a word. No one knew what to say but I could now see the concern in their eyes and it gave me some hope. At least we had someone behind us because we knew this was only the beginning.

Instead of talking outside, MJ unlocked the door and we all went inside. I pushed Veronica's chair to the living room and told the kids to get a snack and head down to the home theatre. We would talk with them later once we wrapped our minds around the situation at hand.

"If y'all are here to condemn me too then you can save it. I've had enough condemnation to last me a lifetime," Veronica said as I helped her out of the wheelchair and onto the sofa. She was not only physically tired but I now knew her spirit was tired.

"That's not why we're here. We know that's not who you are anymore Veronica," Torre said with tears threatening to fall from her eyes.

"Ronnie we are here for support. We may not be blood but we are family," Malachi said putting his hand on my shoulder.

"We really appreciate that. This is going to be a long road ahead of us trying to clear up this mess," I said still watching Veronica break.

Before anyone else could say anything Destiny came into the room, carrying her iPad, shaking her head.

"What's wrong princess?" I asked as she walked over to me and handed the device to me. Looking down and reading the headlines infuriated me. As bad as I didn't want to show Veronica I knew she would eventually find out. The tabloids and gossip blogs had gotten wind of the story and it had only come out less than an hour ago.

"PULPIT PIMPTRESS? FIRST LADY VERONICA MILLHOUSE USED TO BE A PIMP!"

"SAY WHAT NOW? FIRST LADY HAD A FIRST LADY?"

"PRAYING AND PIMPING...IS THIS WHAT THE BIBLE TEACHES?"

"LADY OF THE CLOTH OR LADY OF THE NIGHT?"

Destiny had pulled up different web pages and each headline seemed to be worse than the last. Malachi and Torre looked over my shoulder and the tears she was holding previously began to fall.

"Dez go ahead back downstairs and stay off of the web for now until we can figure things out" I told her as she nodded her head and walked over to give her mother a hug. Veronica must have thought the kids would be upset with her because the relief that showed on her face at that moment looked like that's what she needed.

Once Destiny was finally out of the room she said, "I guess I should let you know how all of this started."

"Ronnie that's not necessary," Torre tried to stop her.

"Yes it is. If you stand beside us I want you to know what you're getting into. You will be looked down on for standing by us and I don't want that. You already have to deal with the pregnancy and it's selfish for me to ask that you focus on this too," she said, always looking out for other's interest before hers.

"No matter what you tell us we are here for you," Malachi said taking a seat. He knew this was about to be a rough one.

****

Twenty Five Years Ago

"Alright now baby girl, it's show time," my father said. I was fifteen years old and had finally reached the age to where he thought I was old enough to learn the family business as he called it. My mother had abandoned us when I was seven years old. She left one day saying she was going to the store and never came back. It wasn't until years later that I found out why she had left us.

Anyway, all I had ever seen were different men and women coming in and out of the house at all times of the night and I never knew why my father Clarence never let any of them around me. When they would come over he would send me in my room. Every now and then I would peek my head out of my room or even ease my way to the end of the hall and eavesdrop. I never heard anything out of the ordinary but I knew that tons of money was being brought in.

I always had the best of everything. All of the latest shoes, clothes, toys, any and everything that my heart desired, I got. When I asked him where he got all of the money from he told me that once I got older he would teach me the family business. I was confused because he never left the house to go to work anywhere so what type of business was he running? I assumed that the people coming in and out were his employees and to a certain extent, they were; well the women anyway.

He would always tell me that when I was older I would start running it myself, so on the night of my fifteenth birthday I started my "job". We pulled up on the side of the road in Englewood, one of the rougher neighborhoods in Chicago.

"You see that woman over there?" he asked as he pointed to a woman who looked thin as a rail and I could only imagine what she smelled like. Her hair was matted down and the outfit she had on was way too big for her

small frame. Her light brown skin looked pale and her hazel eyes were sunken into her head. If she wasn't moving I would have thought that she was dead. I'm sure she must have felt that way but with every passing car that stopped at the stop sign, she was trying to get the driver to allow her access.

"Yea, what about her?" I asked him looking confused.

"Go over there and hand her this," he said as he handed me a hundred dollar bill.

"Do you know her? Why are you giving her our money?"

The look he gave me let me know that I should stop asking questions and do as I was told so I shut up, took the money, and reached for the door handle.

"When you give it to her let her know it's more where that came from and if she's smart she'll come hop in the back seat. Let her know that she has five minutes to

make a decision or I'm pulling off," he said starting the car again.

Walking across the street I finally paid attention to my surroundings and noticed that there were at least ten other women out there who were dressed to the nines and they were doing the same thing this woman was doing. The only difference between them and her - they were getting in and out of multiple cars while this one was steady begging. Pathetic I thought to myself. It didn't take a rocket scientist to figure out what was going on and even at the young age I was, I understood.

Tapping her on her shoulder, she turned around looking scared out of her mind. "Here," I said handing her the money. She looked skeptical at first but slowly reached out her hand to take it. Before she could snatch it and run I firmly told her,

"There's more where this came from if you come with me. But if you don't you better believe that we will come back for this plus interest and I would hate for you not to have it. It doesn't seem like you have any customers

as it is," I said to her letting her know I knew what she was up to and how she wasn't getting paid. No my father didn't tell me to say all of that but if I was to run this business then I was going to make sure I got the job done.

Before I could make it back to the car home girl had beat me and was getting in the back seat. My father looked at me like he was impressed as he pulled off. It took about a week to get Lacy ready to be back on the block but when she did, she outshined everyone that was in the hood. Before the night was over she had brought in over twenty five hundred dollars and I was scoping out my next recruit.

Three years later Clarence and his daughter Ron were the talk of Chicago and not always in a good way. Some felt he was taking their business with the women that he put out there but it was a dog eat dog world and he was going to make sure we ate better than everybody else.

One night after we had put all of our women out on their streets we stopped to get something to eat. While I waited in the car I watched as this couple began arguing a few cars down from where I was. The girl looked to be around my age and everything about her intrigued me. Her hair and makeup was flawless and her outfit left nothing to the imagination. As I watched her there was just something about her that gave me this tingling feeling that was unexplainable.

I had never been with anyone willingly but I knew what I was feeling although I knew it was all kinds of wrong; but it just felt so right. My dad got back in the car and was about to pull off when I stopped him. I didn't say a word as I nodded my head in their direction. Putting the car back in park and turning off the ignition he sat back and watched the show.

I knew the wheels were turning in his head on how to make this girl work for him but I was busy planning how I would get her to be with me. I had never been in a relationship with a woman and this would be a first for me. Just as soon as the thought crossed my mind we saw the man raise his hand and punch her square in her face.

"HEY!" I yelled jumping out of the car with my father hot on my heels. The girl's nose was bleeding as she broke out crying and my dad ran up on her dude with his gun locked and loaded.

Instead of saying anything he raised his hands in surrender because he already knew what time it was. No one crossed Uncle Clarence as the women called him, but the look on his face said that this was far from over. I grabbed her hand and led her back to the car as I watched my father give ole boy the worst beating of his life.

I had seen plenty men catch a beat down from my father more times than I could count but never this bad. I got in the back seat and tried to clean her up the best I could with the napkins that had come with our meal. It felt like the more I wiped her nose the more she bled.

"Thank you," she said to me. All I did was nod my head and continue cleaning her up as best as I could.

"My name is-" I started but she cut me off.

"Ron. I know. I've had my eye on you for a while now. I'm Iesha but everyone calls me E," she said.

My dad came back to the car and pulled off. We didn't go back to our house on the other side of town, but we went to the spot where we let the girls lay their heads. I got her some clothes together and was about to leave when she pulled me close for a kiss."

Chapter Fourteen

Veronica

Going over the details of what led me up to this moment were hard to go over again. I felt so bad that Marcus had to sit here and listen to it another time. God knows I didn't want to put myself through this again, let alone him. I looked around the room and everyone seemed to have the same weary looks on their faces. I thought maybe they would feel like I felt and be disgusted but none of them showed any signs of that.

"So she ended up being your girlfriend?" Malachi asked.

Looking down I softly said, "Yeah. I had never been with a woman before willingly. I mean a few times some of the women would rub their bodies up against me and I didn't like it at all. That's why I was surprised at the feelings I was having towards Iesha."

"You know how the enemy works. He presents things to us that aren't right and deep down we know it's wrong but the way he packages it up makes it feel so right," Torre said.

"You're absolutely right. We have to be careful what we subject ourselves to, and not all the time is it easy," Marcus agreed.

"So why is Iesha so bent on making your life a living hell now after all of these years?" Malachi asked.

I closed my eyes and took a deep breath before continuing.

"Almost a year after meeting Iesha I started to cut back on having her out on the block. So one night my dad had us go out recruiting while he went to collect the money from the other women. When he got over to Englewood he saw Iesha's old pimp Bean all up in one of our worker's face trying to get the money she had on her for the night. He felt like ever since my dad had taken Iesha from him he wasn't making as much money and she continued to stay fly.

As soon as my dad got up on him he realized it was a set up. Some of the girls felt like he was picking favorites and once Bean got in their heads even more, it was easy to convince them to turn on Clarence. Bean was able to find out his schedule for pickups and even where they lived.

After a brief struggle, two shots rang out back-to-back. The women scattered and when the dust cleared both my father and Bean lie dead in the middle of the street. They had both pulled their guns on the other and lost their lives in the middle of their sins. Once word got back to me I lost it. I vowed to make everyone pay that was involved. But I wasn't a killer. I couldn't find it in me to take the life of someone else.

What I didn't expect was that Iesha was a part of the whole plan. From the very beginning she knew that my father was going to be set up. Bean felt that if they could get rid of my father then he could get his streets back. But none of us had planned on me and Iesha falling for one another.

By now I was livid. The woman that I had saved and ended up giving my body to was the reason that my father was dead. Although I couldn't kill her I was set on making her pay, so I pimped her out like she had never been pimped before. She had no idea that I found out what she had done. The love that I once thought was real for her was now long gone and I had nothing but hate in my heart, but unbeknownst to me the love she had was growing.

I would talk to her any kind of way, calling her out of her name, and beating her if she tried to come up short with the money she owed; just real disrespectful to her. I saw my father do it to the women on a regular basis so I kicked it up a notch on her. I just wanted her to pay for my father's death.

Then one day I couldn't find her. I searched high and low on every side of town that I could and still came up with nothing. Then finally I went to her parent's house. I had been there plenty of times but never stayed too long or made much eye contact. There was something about her mother Mrs. Verna that told me she could see right through me.

Knocking on the door I waited for someone to answer. I was ready to get Iesha and get home to deal with her accordingly.

"Is E here?" I asked as soon as Mrs. Verna opened the door. There was no need for pleasantries.

"Um, hi Veronica. Come on in baby and have a seat," she said.

"Nah that's ok. Is she here or not because I have some things I need to get back to," I said letting her know that I didn't have time to play these games with her today, and I didn't know why she insisted on calling me Veronica.

"Please, just for a few minutes. I need to let you know what's going on. I promise not to keep you long."

Realizing that she wouldn't let me leave without talking I decided to go ahead and get it over with. The further I walked into the house the more I felt like weight was being lifted off of me. Before I had gone in I had felt so heavy and didn't know why.

"Veronica, I know this isn't the life that you want but it's the one that was dealt to you. Sometimes situations we are exposed to won't allow us to go in a different direction," she started.

Something in me wanted to run out of there but it was as if I was glued to the seat because I literally could not move. I guess she thought she'd better hurry up before I was able to get up, so she continued.

"Ever since Iesha was born her father and I knew there was something wrong. We took her to every specialist we could and tried to get her all of the help we could find for her. I even made sure to give her a little more attention than I did her sister and brother. Not because I loved her more, but I understood that something wasn't quite right.

As far as I could remember she has been acting out, rebelling against us no matter how much we tried loving her. She was failing in school so bad she was moved to one of the special classes in the middle of the school. That seemed to only make things worse because by the time she entered high school, she had been kicked out of every alternative school that was available.

Eventually we had to get her admitted to get some help and that worked for a while. But then one day she met that man Bean she was fooling around with and fell right back into her same routine."

"Why are you telling me all of this?" I asked starting to get annoyed as well as a little frightened. It sounded

like Mrs. Verna was telling me that her child needed to be in a loony bin.

"I'm telling you this because since the first time I met you I knew this wasn't the lifestyle that you wanted to live. I just felt that you had no choice and got caught up. I don't want this life to hold you hostage to the point where you are unable to get out. I pray for you every night I pray for the rest of my family because I see where you can go if you leave this life that you're living.

There is nothing in these streets but death. Not just physical death but death of your spirit and that can be the worst kind of death to suffer. The reason you can't find Iesha is because she had to be admitted into the hospital. She had stopped taking her medicine and she has missed her last four appointments with her therapist. It was for her own safety and possibly the safety of others," she finished.

I didn't know what was going on but I had to get out of there. I couldn't take this and needed some fresh air. The woman that I had fallen in love with had not only plotted against my father and gotten him killed, but she was crazy as hell!

I don't know how I got home because the last thing I remember is Mrs. Verna saying something about trusting God. I had no clue on how to even begin talking to God especially with the things I had been doing. There was no way He was listening to me, or so I thought. As I walked into the condo that we had been living in, I looked around at all of the elaborate furniture, electronics, clothes, shoes, just things that we had and felt nothing but defeat. The life I had been living had me feeling defeated and I was tired.

"Are you ready?" I heard. It was as clear as day but I was the only one in the house. The tears started falling from my eyes and I didn't even try stopping them. I felt like I needed this release. So many years of just going through the motions of what I thought was the life and hadn't even begun to live. I was dying without even having the chance of knowing what it was like to really live.

So I surrendered. I knew the voice of God was the one that I had heard and I knew what I had to do. I fell on my face and cried out to Him. I asked Him if I needed to walk away to please show me how, and He did. After what felt like days of me crying, and releasing everything that was not of God that I had in me, I packed my clothes, took enough money to get a bus ticket and a hotel for a month, and I waited.

Two days later when Iesha came in, the house was full of God's spirit. I knew He had forgiven me for every single sin that I had committed and He was allowing me to get ready to begin living. I had the worship music going and although I was crying, these were now tears of joy. I had my bags packed and when she entered the room I waited for my sign from God.

She thought I was crying because I was worried about her and she fell at my feet. I looked at her and said, "I'm leaving."

You could have knocked her over with a feather at that moment but I didn't care. I had already asked God for a sign that let me know what I was doing was right and with the next words that left her mouth I knew.

"Leave? Why? Is it something I did? Are you upset that I went out of town? I was going to ask your permission but I had to go right away. I'm so sorry I will never leave your side again. Tell me how to fix this," she continued on.

At that moment I knew that because she couldn't tell me the truth about where she had been I needed to leave. Sometimes we look for God to give us big signs that we need to leave a situation behind before we do, but He's already given us instructions yet we refuse to listen. We think they are too small to be from God so we wait around for the big signs that never come and then it's too late. I didn't want it to be too late for me.

"I can't live like this anymore. This isn't me. This isn't the life God planned for me. I had time to think while I was here alone and I was finally able to hear the voice of God speak to me. I knew if I didn't give my life over to Him

right then, there was no way of escape for me." I told her. I was done.

"So she didn't try to stop you?" asked Malachi. He looked like he had been holding his breath the whole time I was talking.

"No. But-" I began and stopped as my mind went back to her final words as I was leaving out.

"But what?" Marcus asked. When I was telling him the other day about my past this one thing didn't come to my mind.

"As I was leaving I heard her say, 'You'll be sorry!' I never thought anything else of it, I just thought she was saying that as a scorned lover. And after so many years had gone by I hadn't thought about it anymore."

"Well I guess she made good on her threat. Something is telling me that she isn't done just yet though," Torre said before the doorbell rang.

Chapter Fifteen

Mrs. Verna

I could not believe what I had just witnessed. My child had just put one of the most well known First Ladies of our time on blast in front of the whole church. Not only that, but their church broadcasts their services online for the world to see.

I could only imagine what was going through everybody's minds at that moment. I knew there was a reason that Iesha had moved on such short notice. It had nothing to do with a new job but had everything to do with her seeking revenge on Veronica.

Lord knows I remember the last conversation I had with her before she left. Even before I had gotten the opportunity to reveal everything with her, God had showed me who she really was and that at the time I'm sure Veronica had no clue the greatness that was in her. No matter how happy they said they made each other I could tell that it wasn't in Veronica's heart. That's not who she was. Circumstances at the time caused her to do something that she never would have normally.

Iesha on the other hand I knew she was a little touched. Always has been, even at birth. As soon as she was born I looked in her eyes and knew something wasn't right. That's why I had always tried to give her more attention than my other two children. Not because I didn't love them, because our children were all loved the same way, but because I felt that if I could show her that she was special then maybe whatever in her would not manifest into something bigger. I guess that didn't work.

"My Lord. What are we going to do?" my husband Bernard said to me as we sat and watched the mayhem unfold.

Since that was a rhetorical question I didn't even bother answering him. When Iesha called and told us that she had been attending Clover Hill I immediately started missing our own services so that we could stream into theirs. I felt in my spirit something was up because no matter how many times I kept trying to tell myself that nothing was wrong and I was overreacting, God wouldn't let me rest.

Although I tried to get to Atlanta every chance I got, I knew this trip would be everything but a vacation.

Before I had time to get all of my thoughts together Bernard said to me, "Go pack while I purchase our tickets and get the itinerary."

If anyone knew me it was that man right there. After forty six years of marriage he knew me like the back of his hand and was always ready to do what was necessary to make sure home was taken care of. I kissed him before heading to our room to pack our bags.

****

Iesha

Now that I had let the lion out of the jungle all I had to do was sit back and wait. I knew once Veronica's flock knew what she had been up to they would turn on her in a heartbeat. That's just how these church folk were. They were all "Praise God" this, and "Hallelujah" that, when most of them just went to church to put on a show. And the worst were the leaders. I knew that Marcus was going to leave Veronica when he found out her secret. I could tell by the look on his face when I dropped that bomb that he had no clue about her previous lifestyle.

Baby they ran up out of that church so fast all you could see was smoke. At first I felt bad about dropping the bomb that their precious son had gotten his girlfriend pregnant, but that just made it a more interesting show to put on. I bet you're wondering how I knew that little tidbit, huh? That's not important right now. I'll tell you later once I get my meddling mother off the phone. I looked down at my cell and took a deep breath to prepare myself for this lecture.

"Hey Mommy!" I said trying to sound upbeat like I haven't just created a new series called 'Love and Church Folks Atlanta.' Mona Scott

Young could learn a thing or two from me with this one. Before I got too caught up on the new reality show idea my father's voice brought me back to my reality.

"Iesha! What in the world have you done?" he yelled at me. I should have known if I went too far he would be the one to chastise me. I don't know why I told them what church I was attending when he asked me a few weeks ago. I should have kept my mouth shut.

"Hey Daddy! What are you talking about?" I asked playing dumb but failing miserably.

He chuckled before he answered me so I knew he was mad. "Have you not been watching the news?" he asked way too calmly. I would have just preferred he yell at me and get it over with. I had things I needed to do.

"No I haven't." I answered honestly. TV was not on my agenda right now; I had other matters at hand to take care of.

"Well maybe you should turn it on," he said, more of a demand than a request.

Not sure if I could get anymore on his wrong side than I was right now, I got up and turned on the hotel television. As soon as I did the biggest smile I had ever had came across my face. There as breaking news was the story of Veronica and I. I had made national news!

"You better fix it before I do," my father said not waiting for me to reply as he hung up the phone.

I didn't care what threats he was making. To me they were idle considering he was in Chicago. Had I been back home I knew how my parents would "fix" the situation and I had no intentions of going back to Mercy Hospital anytime soon.

After I finished watching the news and how the media was tearing Veronica and her precious life apart, I turned the TV off and stripped before getting in bed. I turned off my cell phone and started to get comfortable when there was a knock at the door.

"What the hell?" I said looking out of the peephole and snatching the door open.

"What are you doing here Patrick?" I asked pulling him inside and checking to make sure no one was following him.

“Don’t worry, I’m alone and I’m here for my payment,” he said already knowing what my next questions would be.

Detective Patrick Johannsen had been one of my most loyal johns back in the Chi. I met him when he was a street cop and instead of dragging me downtown to jail I provided him with my services. Veronica didn’t know what was going on between us even though there were no feelings involved, I kept him around just in case I would need him to help me out a jam one day. That day had come.

Once Veronica left Chicago I had no idea where she had gone, so I used what I had to get what I wanted. I had more than enough money to survive for a long time; even the rest of my life had I spent it right, but none of that mattered if I couldn’t share it with Ron, so I asked Patrick to help me find her. It took him years to locate her and I was just about to cut him off when we got our big break.

To find out that she had moved on, gotten married, and was now living this holy lifestyle had me heated. I vowed to myself right then I would get her back, or at least tear her world up while trying.

Patrick's voice brought me back to the present.

"Where is my money E?" he asked me looking like he was irritated. He had some nerve.

Moving in close and invading his personal space I said,

"When the job is complete and I have Ron back then you will get the rest of your money. If you mess up this plan you can forget about any further payments and your career will be down the drain."

He had some nerve coming in here trying to act like he was bout that life demanding money from me like I was his trick. It was the other way around and he had no clue yet.

"Mess up this plan?" he mocked me. "You have done that all by yourself. What part of the plan was it that you would out Veronica where the whole world would see it?" His round face was starting to turn the color of a ripe red tomato and I knew he was pissed.

I hadn't thought about the consequences of what I had done. I just wanted her to hurt like I hurt when she left, and for her to come back to me so we could comfort each other.

"Do you not realize now that everyone knows they are going to start investigating? You know the media loves stuff like this," he said.

It had never crossed my mind that if someone got to digging around, they would find the connection between Patrick and I and the rest of the plan we had hatched out. Although I was starting to panic on the inside I had to keep it together on the outside and make sure Patrick remained calm.

"I'm sorry daddy. You're right. Forgive me?" I purred in his ear. I could tell that I was getting to him and no matter how tough he tried to act he was just a weak mutt who I know God couldn't have had a purpose for in life.

Without saying another word I reminded him why he fell for me in the first place as I thought about how to clean up this mess and get my woman back.

Chapter Sixteen

Marcus

It felt like we had been in the house for months when it had only been a few days. The tension in the house was so thick you had to use an axe to cut through it. I tried my best to make sure our home environment was a peaceful one but with the news crews staked out in front of our house, the phones ringing off the hook, and the media stories not calming down, I was at a loss.

After Veronica finished reliving her past again the other day, there was a knock on the door. When I went to go answer it I was met with a swarm of reporters throwing questions at me left and right. The flash of the cameras were blinding and at that moment I knew I couldn't fix this. We needed God for a miracle. Malachi and his family could barely get in their car to drive home without being attacked with questions like "Is this the kind of family you want to be associated with?" and "How does it feel to know that the grandmother of your child is a hypocritical lesbian?"

I promise to God had I not been saved and loved Him like I do I would have let the old Marcus body that reporter where he stood for coming out of his mouth like that.

I went to check on Veronica in our bedroom, and she had finally taken my advice about taking something so that she could get some rest. I knew this was not just hard on her physical body, but her spiritual man was in a war as well. I laid my hand on her head after reaching beside the bed and grabbing the bottle of anointing oil and put some on my hand. I began to pray,

"Father I come to you right now hurting. I hurt for my wife, God. The wonderful woman that you presented to me needs me and I don't know what to do to help her. I know she still has faith in you, dear Lord, but I can see she is getting tired. Let me be that strength for her and our children. Give strength and understanding even to the ones that are turning their backs on us during this time. They don't fully understand and some may not even want to understand. You know people can be so judgmental and revel in the hurt of other's pain, but I pray for them right now.

As I lay hands on my beautiful wife I pray that the chains that held her bound are permanently broken. This may have been the way that you saw fit for her to be free by revealing this secret. God you know that it hurts, but we do understand that even the most precious diamonds have to go through a pressing to come out shining in the end. Help us to endure the pressure and not fall under it. Let our children be not effected more than they already have, and give them a peace that surpasses all understanding.

Lord, keep us close to your bosom and protected from further harm. Remove the shame that we are all feeling and help us to hold our heads up high. I don't know if I should even ask you this Father, but everyone that was involved I pray receive the punishment that they deserve for the pain they have caused. Let them feel your wrath because your word says in Psalms 'to touch not your anointed and do your prophets no harm.' I believe in your word and I know that it will not come back to you void. Have your way in this situation and let your will be done for us all. In Jesus' mighty name I pray, Amen."

I finished praying for her and walked out of the room. I was tired but I had to make sure my family was okay first. I didn't hear the kids upstairs so I figured they had to have been in the theatre room. I was glad that even though we were going through one of the worst times in our lives as a family, they were holding their heads up high. They made sure to not only tell their mother how much they loved her and supported her, but they showed her. I know that gave Veronica just a little bit of peace.

"Hey daddy," the twins said at the same time as I stuck my head in the room. I always wondered what made twins do that.

"Hey babies," I said walking in and flopping down beside MJ who was on his phone with Lailani.

"You alright dad?" MJ asked, stopping his FaceTime conversation.

"Hi Mr. Marcus. How is Mrs. Veronica?" Lailani asked with a worried expression on her pretty little face.

"Hey sweetheart. I'm okay and she's resting finally. How are you feeling?" I asked her. This first trimester was kicking her butt. It was still hard for me to believe that I was about to become a grandfather and my sixteen year old son was headed to fatherhood, but I knew I had to be there for them. They made a mistake but there was going to be such a beautiful blessing that came from it, although I know my lecture that I gave MJ was enough to make him not want any more kids until he was married and on his own.

"I'm a little better. I can finally eat now and keep it down. This sickness is the worst," she said.

"Is it safe to say that you have learned your lesson?" I asked looking from the phone to MJ.

"YES!" everyone in the room said including the twins. I wasn't worried about them because they would be on lockdown until they were fifty if I had my way.

"Good. I'm going to order some dinner and I'll call you when it arrives," I said to them, walking out of the room. I didn't notice that Destiny was behind me until I made it back upstairs to the kitchen to find the take out menus.

"Daddy?" she said.

Turning around I replied, "Yea Dezzy baby, what's up?" I found the menu I was looking for and grabbed the house phone.

"Was mommy born that way?" she asked throwing me off.

"Why do you ask that?"

"Well I've heard some of the girls and boys at my school that live that lifestyle say they were born that way. That that was the way God made them," she answered.

"Come sit down with me sweetie," I said walking over to the kitchen table. Before I could answer her Veronica entered.

She was able to get around a little better at home now even with the cast on her leg. Sitting down beside us she said, "Those kids are right in a sense. Do I believe that some people are born that way? Yes. Do I think that God made them like that? No. Do I think that God still loves them? Absolutely. God loves us all but He said nothing about liking what it is we do when it doesn't line up with His word," she began explaining.

"But how can people be born like that?" Destiny asked.

"Well I believe certain seeds are already planted in some of us because of the sin of others before us.

Remember when we talked about generational curses at church and how what we do may not affect us directly or right away, but could affect our children or our grandchildren and so on?" Veronica asked.

"Yes ma'am," Dez responded.

"That's why we have to be very careful of the life we live. The life I lived before I gave my life over to God was one that I thought I would live forever. I was having the time of my life but there were days where I knew it was wrong. And on those days I would push the thought to the back of my mind and kept doing me. I wanted to be in control of my life. The way I was living was the only way that I knew how to survive. That seed was planted already because of what my father had instilled in me.

He was the one that exposed me to the fast life, quick money, even the women. Because I didn't have my mother there to guide me, my father was my only example. Yes he loved me, but he didn't know how to raise me to be a good woman. He could only give me what he had and nothing more. That's why when God stepped in to get me I made a promise that when I was blessed with children I would raise you the best that I could with the tools God gave me to use."

"Baby girl, God is a gentleman. He won't make us do anything that we don't want to do. He loves us all no matter what our faults are but He doesn't like the sinful ways of the world that we have adapted. Can I say that all homosexuals will go to hell? No I can't because I don't know what that person's last conversation will be like with God before they leave this earth. I don't know the personal relationship they have so it's not my place to cast judgment on anyone. I just love all of God's people and we want you to do the same. Just because your personal beliefs may be different from another's does not mean you should turn your nose up at them. You continue to walk in love with each other," I said.

"That makes sense. So it's ok to be friends with them?" she asked.

"Of course, Dez. As long as they are not trying to make you do something you don't want to do then it's absolutely nothing wrong with being friends. Who knows, you may be that one person that God uses to get them closer to Him," Veronica said.

We talked a little while more before Destiny went back to join her siblings while we waited on dinner. If there was nothing else she took with her after this conversation, we hoped she got the point to just love people the way God loves us.

Chapter Seventeen

Veronica

Finally the media had calmed down a bit and we were able to leave the house and not get swamped by the news crews. Marcus and I had just left the doctor's office getting that awful cast removed. I had had that thing on so long that my leg looked twice as small as the other one. I didn't care though; I was healed and able to walk again.

As we were pulling out of the parking lot Marcus's phone rang. It was Malachi calling. We knew that they had taken Lay to her appointment and we were hoping that they were calling to let us know what we were having. There were days where we were still trying to adjust to that news but so far we were handling it well as a family.

We had all wanted to be there with her to celebrate but since it took longer than expected to remove my cast, MJ was the only one who could make it.

"What's going on Malachi? What are we having?" I heard Marcus say.

"Man, we don't know. The baby wasn't in a position where we could see," he responded sounding disappointed.

"That's my girl! Already she's making sure to keep herself covered," I said knowing in my heart it was a girl.

"Maybe *my boy* doesn't want everyone up in his business," Marcus said as I rolled my eyes.

"Anyway, the other reason I called was to see what's going on at the church. I don't remember you saying anything about any services coming up since you were taking a break," he said confusing both Marcus and myself.

"We don't have any services and no one should be there besides the normal everyday staff," I said looking over at Marcus. He had already gotten in the lane to make a U-turn so we could head back in the direction of the church.

"Where are you? We're on our way," Marcus said.

"We turned around and are pulling back into the parking lot of the church."

"Wait for us before you go in."

"Okay. See you in a few," Malachi said hanging up the phone. I had a feeling things were about to get real.

Eight minutes later we were pulling into the lot of the church we started and were shocked to see about thirty of our member's cars gathered. It wasn't a day where we normally had prayer and after the events of the last few weeks, we felt it was best to shut things down. Home was our first ministry and right now was our priority. We couldn't be productive for anyone else if we weren't productive for our family.

We had the kids wait outside just in case something was about to jump off, as I felt it would. We didn't need them stressing out again, especially Lailani. I held on to Marcus as the four of us walked making sure to steady myself since my leg was just a little on the weak side following the cast removal.

As we opened the door to the sanctuary, everyone that was filling up the first three pews in front of the church turned to look at us. We heard a few mumbles and saw a few smiles and relieved faces. This was definitely a house divided I felt. And we all know that a house that is divided was one that could not stand. Jesus be a fence!

"Well look what we have here. If it isn't Pastor and the First *Lesbian"* said Sister Monique.

"Okay, what we are not gonna do is be disrespectful up in the Lord's house," I said.

"Ooohhh, so now you're concerned with the Lord. Were you so concerned with the Lord when you were spreading it-"

"MONIQUE!" yelled Mother Wanda cutting her off. "Say another disrespectful word in God's house and so help me Jesus we gonna turn up!" she said standing up. Her husband Deacon Harris gently placed his hand on her arm to get her to calm down. Had the situation not been so serious that would have been the funniest thing I had ever witnessed, but this was no laughing matter.

"What's going on here?" Marcus asked.

Deacon Harris stood up to fill us in. "Well a few of the members felt like you and First Lady needed to step down from your positions as head pastor and assistant pastor. I told them that was impossible since it was the two of you who started the church. If they felt that way then they should just go somewhere else."

"And we said that we were not the ones who were misleading people and shouldn't have to go anywhere, we belong here," said Monique with about twenty others in agreement with her.

"So what you're saying is they don't belong here?" asked Torre.

"Them nor you. What kind of example are you setting for our youth? That it's ok to sleep with the same sex and degrade women for a dollar, or to have premarital sex and have a baby out of wedlock? Some examples y'all are," said Nyeema. She was one of the youth volunteers.

"Now wait a minute, let me make sure I got this straight. You're saying that we are bad examples for the youth but what example are you setting by having three baby daddies and still no husband for those little snotty nosed heathens you got running around here every week? Go head, I'll wait," said Torre folding her arms across her chest and tapping her foot on the floor.

You smell that? That is the smell of you know what's officially hitting the fan and that thing was blowing on high.

As wrong as that may have been I understood where Torre was coming from and it shut Nyeema right on up. You can't call the kettle black if your pot was the same shade.

"Look, this is not a time to go against one another. This is a time that we need to be standing beside and with each other," said Deacon Harris getting a few amen's on his side. It looked like we were getting ready to be on trial for a crime that God hadn't found us guilty in.

It always amazed me when the "church folks" were the ones pointing their fingers and rolling their eyes more than the ones who had yet come to Christ. Then they wondered why churches aren't growing. Who wants to be a part of something that says they represent God but their actions prove them wrong? That's exactly why people have what we call "church hurt." Who could blame them?

"Listen, the life my wife lived prior to me and this ministry has nothing to do with the person she is today," Marcus said in my defense.

"That's a lie! It has everything to do with her sitting up here each week telling us what *thus said the Lord* but she was out here living everything but the word of God," another one of our members Deacon Jones said. That one threw us for a loop because if anyone had known the type of people Marcus and I were, it would be him. He was here since the doors opened five years ago.

I shook my head as I thought about the overtime the enemy was putting in to have people turn against us. I was tired but I had to fight.

"The keyword Deacon Jones is *was*. What did you feel about me when you were coming to Marcus and I needing help with your bills that got behind due to your gambling addiction? Did the Lord tell you not to take our money because it came from my past lifestyle? I mean you have this direct line to God and everything so I'm sure He told you, *'Don't you dare take that money from them Deacon Jones. That's dirty money Veronica had from over twenty years ago that she got from pimpin' hoes*!" I said. I know that may not have been real "First Lady-ish" but I was done letting people continue to attack my character when all I wanted to do was serve God's people.

In the words of Mother Harris, I bet he got somewhere and sot down then. Before I went in any further on ole Deacon Jones, Sister Monique looked like she wanted to get in on it, too. Oh I had enough tea to pour and shade to throw if she wanted to go there. I may have been First Lady Veronica Millhouse but I had yet to make it to the pearly gates so that meant I had some work that needed to be done. I was not all the way delivered just yet.

As soon as she opened her mouth the doors to the church were opened and we were not extending the right hand of fellowship at this particular moment. Everyone turned to face the back of the church as I prepared for this long overdue battle.

"Torre hold my earrings," I said taking them off and sliding out of my flats. If Iesha wanted a piece of me she was about to get it.

I looked over at Torre and she was pulling her hair back while making sure her sneakers were tightly tied. We made eye contact as I said, "Father, please forgive us."

Chapter Eighteen

Iesha

"That's right Pastor, you better hold her back!" I taunted as Marcus grabbed Veronica by her waist. I had to commend him for being so strong cause Veronica was far from huge but she was a long way from being a small woman. If you were gonna hold her back you had to have some strength behind you. I saw plenty of women catch the beat down when they didn't have what was owed to her. I knew had it not been for Marcus being there I would have caught a quick two piece.

And who was this ole red broad that thought she was gonna jump bad? I got mad thinking that this is who Ron replaced me with so I flat out asked.

"Oh this you?" I said imitating the line from the movie ATL when Rashad's ex girl came for New New. Maybe that wasn't redbone's favorite movie or something because that comment allowed her to break free for a split second and catch me right in my mouth.

I put my hand up to my mouth and when I pulled it away I saw nothing but blood. So this is the way they wanted to do it in the Lord's house? It was show time.

From the way everyone's eyes grew wide, I knew I had their attention when I pulled out my custom made purple berretta. I just loved how the gun fit perfectly in my hand. And thanks to all of the times Veronica took me to the shooting range, I was a pretty good shot.

The looks on their faces went from scared to confused once Detective Johansen walked in and stood beside me.

"I knew something wasn't right about him, I could feel it in the hospital," Marcus said.

"I knew something wasn't right about him I could feel it in the hospital," I mocked. "Oh shut up Marcus. If you knew so much you would have known your wife was a good for nothing whore who got pleasure out of making women fall for her and then making them feel worthless!" I said raising my voice as Patrick walked beside me down the aisle. It was right comical like we were about to say our wedding vows.

I saw the expression on Marcus's face change and I knew that I had landed on a gold mine.

"Oh, you didn't know I wasn't the only lover the sweet and pure First Lady had? There were plenty others, but I was special. Well at least that's what I was told." I could care less about the tears falling down her face at that moment.

"You know that wasn't true!" Veronica shouted.

"What I know is there was me, Angelica, Sabrina, and Tanya. There could have been more that I was unaware of but that's okay. I knew I was your main chick."

Veronica looked like she was about to up chuck everything she had eaten the last two months at the sound of the names I had just called out. Okay, maybe they weren't really her other lovers. They were some of the women who her father allowed to have their way with her when she was younger. He called himself prepping her for her position. From the look on Marcus's face he had no idea who I was talking about so it just made for better story telling.

"Iesha you know who they were. I told you who they were and what they did to me," she said shaking in her shoes, literally.

"This is true. I do know what they did to you but Ron, didn't I do it better?" I said giving her a smile filled with so much lust Lucifer himself would have been uncomfortable.

"Listen this has been going on long enough! We need to-"

POW!

"Shut up old man!" I said silencing old man Jones for all eternity. I was about to put his old broad out of her misery but it gave me a feeling of euphoria to watch her huddled over her husband crying as he took his last breath.

"Now does anyone else have anything to say? If so speak now or forever hold your peace, like Pops should have," I asked looking around the room.

Not a word was spoken.

"Good. Now let's move forward. I bet you all want to know why it took me so long to come and how I found you. Am I right?" I asked looking around the room.

Everyone slowly nodded their heads as I took a seat on the chair by the alter. They needed to turn the air on cause it was some kind of hot in here. I looked down at my watch and noticed my special quest was late. I guess I had time to answer their questions.

"Well you see after you left me that day Ron, I cried for what felt like months. One day good ole mother Verna came to the house to check on me. She told me that she had talked to you and told you that I wasn't really visiting family but I was in Mercy. I knew right then at that moment if I didn't get myself together she was going to put me right back in there. So I had to put my game face on.

I started taking my meds like I was supposed to. I was going to church with her every Sunday and spending family time. Everything that was asked of me, I did to a tee. About five or six years after being the perfect little daughter, I came across this hot cop from back in the day although now, he was Detective Johansen so he had a little more clout.

Come to find out he had been looking for me cause no one could make him feel the way I could," I said thinking back on those times we shared together.

"Is this about to be another testimony of yours? Get to the good stuff," Monique said.

POW!

"Didn't your mother tell you to never talk when grown folks are talking? Just disrespectful," I stated calmly as I watched her body hit the floor in a heap.

"Now where was I? Oh yeah. I figured if I planned and waited long enough I could get him to help me find you. I made up this cockamamie story about how I had all of this money that you left me and if he helped me find you I would share it with him. I had blown that money way before he came back into that picture."

"WHAT?!" Patrick yelled startling me. "You mean to tell me I did all of this for nothing? I should lay you out where you stand."

"Sweetie you don't have the balls to do that," I said giving him a look that said to him try me if he wanted to. I watched him as he sat back and realized that the life he thought he was going to happen would never happen. Either he was going to be in jail for the rest of his life or dead after everything was revealed.

"By the time he found you in St. Louis and I had gotten there you were gone again. But not for long. Detective here put in a little overtime and found out that you had relocated here," I continued.

"He even went as far as to transfer to Atlanta so he could be front and center, getting all of the information I needed. Imagine my surprise when he told me you were married to a pastor and that you had children. I told him off gate he was lying and that if you were it was all for a show. There was no way that you would have been happily married, and to a pastor? Nah, not my Ron.

Patrick told me that one of his cute little officers attended church here from time to time, so all of the information that we needed he got from her. What was her name again?" I asked Patrick but before he could open his mouth, in walked my parents.

Chapter Nineteen

Marcus

I couldn't believe what I was seeing and hearing as I stood frozen in place. Two of my members lay dead in the middle of our church and my wife's former lover is crazy and deranged and still continuing to reveal secrets about Veronica's past. The moment the older couple walked in the door it instantly reminded me that our children were still outside. Or were they? Had this psycho done something to them because two shots were already fired and no one had run inside.

I prayed that they were safe and if they were, they were trying to get us some help. I thought my prayer had been answered and that help had come by way of Officer

Norman as she walked into the church right behind the couple. But I quickly put that theory to rest as she walked past everyone right up to the front and gave a quick kiss to Iesha.

"Oh I'm sorry, how rude of me. This is Adrian. Officer Adrian Norman," Iesha said showing all of her teeth and beaming with pride.

"Iesha baby what are you doing?" said the older woman who I learned was her mother. "Did you do all of this? Oh my God Iesha, did you kill these people?" she said running up to Iesha but stopped dead in her tracks as Iesha pointed her gun directly between her mother's eyes.

At that moment I think everyone was holding their breaths. We didn't know if she was going to kill Mrs. Verna, her own mother, or if she was going to allow her to live.

"Please don't do this. We can try and fix this. Don't hurt anyone else," Mrs. Verna pleaded. You could hear the weariness in her voice and knew this was a long battle that she was tired of fighting against her daughter.

"Oh mother, always trying to be the peace maker, Mrs. Fixer upper, if you will."

"Why do you have to keep doing this? Can't you see Veronica is happy with her family and she doesn't want you anymore? This may be your reality but this isn't hers," spoke her father for the first time since entering the church.

"You've done enough harm by outing her to their congregation and God knows how many other people. Please just let it go." Mrs. Verna was now crying as Adrian and Iesha looked at each other as if they were the only ones in the room. They were speaking to each other only through their eyes, no words. Then they turned towards me.

"Well mommy dearest, since I have already exposed Veronica how much fun would it be to expose someone else?" Iesha asked nonchalantly. Although she was speaking to her mother she was looking me dead in my eyes.

"Iesha what are you talking about? What have you done?" her father asked.

"Oh not me," she said shrugging and nodding her head towards me. "Him."

"Me?!" I said not knowing what she was talking about. At that moment I noticed a remote in her hand as she turned on the projector behind me.

There was the back of my chair facing the hidden camera that had been placed in my office and Adrian could be seen just as clear as day unbuttoning her uniform top. She disappeared from the view in front of the chair and I could be heard mumbling.

I dropped my head in shame.

"Looks like First Lady isn't the only one with confessions, huh Pastor?" Iesha said before my world went black.

CPSIA information can be obtained
at www.ICGtesting.com
Printed in the USA
LVOW04s1857040416
482086LV00020B/1101/P